The Medallion
David Huff

Book One

Publisher: David Huff
ISBN: 978-0-9988003-3-2
Library of Congress Control Number: 2018908260
The Medallion/ David Huff
Digital Distribution | David Huff, 2018 Paperback | David Huff | 2018

Dedication

This book is dedicated to all my friends and family who have chosen the path to be the true children of the Great Spirit and be examples to the world of their loyalty to that same Great Spirit. May he always be their guide throughout life now and the hereafter and a shining light to others.

And to John Brewer who discovered the giants of Manti and to his legacy.

"While we are free to choose our actions, we are not free to choose the consequences of those actions. Consequences are governed by natural law.... We can decide to step in front of a fast-moving train, but we cannot decide what will happen when the train hits us." — Stephen R. Covey,

The greatest battles we will ever fight are not on the battlefield in front of others but in front of the mirror, in the dark of night by ourselves when no one is watching.

Chapter I

This is a story that has been handed down through the generations of time. I would suspect most of it is true, but which part of it is, is hard to say. I'll let you be the judge of that for yourselves. This story takes place along the flowing Arkansas River as it feeds through the Royal Gorge of Colorado Territory back in the early 1300s. The river was still untamed by man and the railroad hadn't made its presence known yet and wouldn't for another 500 years. The land was still controlled by the Indians, as the white man or the Spaniards hadn't set foot in this part of the Colorado valley.

The story goes that the Ute Indians, who wintered in the Royal Gorge area, were protecting something down in the valley where the Arkansas River flowed between two mountains that reached the sky and touched the moon. The sacred place, a cave, had been protected for many generations by the Indian tribe whose only purpose was to keep it safe from other tribes, such as the Kiowa, Sioux, Commanche, and Cheyenne, who traveled through the Royal Gorge on their way to hunt buffalo in the southwestern states. They used the Arkansas river as an access point through the canyon to the mountain meadow regions such as the South Park Basin and, in later years, against the Spanish and then white man who would come through the gorge on their way to Utah or New Mexico.

What was in the cave only the shamans or the medicine men knew for sure, but if you knew where the cave was, you could find out for yourself; that is, if you didn't believe in the curse. For the Indians, the place was cursed by the shamans, who were committed to protecting what was in the cave. When the shaman was getting old and ready to die, he would choose one of the courageous Indian braves to take his place and show him where the cave was and what was inside the cave. Once this was done, the old shaman would give the chosen one the medallion that he had worn as a symbol of his duties and responsibilities of being the caretaker of the cave. Part of his responsibilities was to ensure that the tribe would be protected as well. The old shaman would then leave the village in the night and disappear, never to be seen again. This way, only one person at a time would know where and what the secrets of the cave were.

The new shaman was sworn to secrecy and would protect the cave and its contents, even if it meant his life, from anybody who wanted to steal or desecrate it. This also applied to the curious and those that accidently stumbled across it. No one was to know of the location of the cave or its contents except the shaman. He would visit the cave once a year to confirm that all was well as part of his duties.

As time moved on, the cave was forgotten by the Indian tribe who had since been relocated to the Ute Basin Reservation in southern Colorado and New Mexico, and the Uintah and Ouray Reservation in northeastern Utah (The size of the reservation was 3.5 million acres of land, the second largest in the U.S.), far away from the gorge. The last shaman who was the guardian of the cave eventually died on the reservation and no one knows whether he passed on his knowledge or responsibility of the cave or not.

The white man, hearing of the ancient Indian legend, started searching for the cave, but in the end, they never found it, only because it was being protected by the Great Spirit (Su-Noi), who had placed guardians there to keep watch over it, or so the legend says. For many generations, the cave was only thought of as an old Indian legend with no truth to back it up.

And thus, the legend died out with the Indians and was forgotten by all, including the white man who had come hunting for it as well.

The story of the last medicine man starts off with a bear who was a friend to the medicine man and would help him protect the cave, especially when the medicine man slept at night. Their common enemy was the coyote and therefore the medicine man and the bear were always watching out for the coyote because of him being so sneaky. The coyote was the one who always made trouble for the Great Spirit and with the help of the bear the coyote was not able to do much mischief. However, one day when the bear was gone, and the Great Spirit was busy, the coyote sneaked into the cave and took the medallion away from the medicine man as he lay sleeping inside the cave. The coyote chewed on the leather that held the medallion around the medicine man's neck. He took the medallion thinking what mischief he could do with this. When the medicine man woke up, he realized that his medallion was gone and called upon the bear and the Great Spirit to help him find it. The coyote knew he was in trouble because he had made the Great Spirit very angry and feared for his life. So, in order to keep from being destroyed by the Great Spirit or by being eaten by the bear, the coyote took the medallion back to the cave of the medicine man and placed it on the ground in front of the cave. From that point on, the medallion stayed there, not only to protect the cave but also because the medicine man who had lost it now found he was not worthy to wear it again. The medicine man knew he had failed in his duties and cried unto the Great Spirit that he would find favor once again with the Great Spirit. After hearing him cry, the Great Spirit told the medicine man that he would be allowed to be the protector of the cave, but he would not be protected from his enemies, to which the medicine man thanked the Great Spirit in the sky for his benevolence towards him.

Chapter II

Jim was working through the summer on a dig down in the Colorado Royal Gorge area to get enough hours to put towards his doctorate thesis while under the mentorship of his Professor, Dr. Edward Wainwright from Brigham Young University (BYU). Jim had been chosen to go on this dig simply because the Professor liked the young man and because his daughter, Julie, said if he didn't take him, he would have to eat his own cooking while they were out there on the dig. The Professor knew his daughter meant every word and knew that Jim was a good man to have on the dig anyway because of his uncanny ability to find things that average students would overlook in their work, whether it be in the books or on the dig. Jim had a golden touch for finding the unfindable; in fact, the Professor was, in some ways, kind of jealous of Jim's ability for finding things.

Jim had started dating Julie in his second year while he worked on his master's program at the University of Massachusetts. In fact, it was Julie who convinced Jim to continue going after a doctorate at Brigham Young University, coincidentally where her father taught archaeology. Being accepted into the program was rigorous but worthwhile because of the reputation of the school. Once he had been accepted into the program, he had to decide what his doctorate thesis would be in and complete it to show his ideas as proof of why he chose the particular subject to study and write about it and then why it was pertinent to the field of archaeology. With Professor Wainwright as his mentor he was on his way to meeting the basics of his thesis.

Things between Jim and Julie were pretty strong in that they loved each other; in fact, they had planned on getting married after he received his doctorate. Working during the summer with Julie's dad would help in outlining his thesis and give him more time to spend with Julie throughout the summer. Being out in the wilderness under the stars at night would be fun for all involved. The cool nights, listening to the river with your girlfriend, doing what you loved the most, was a great way to spend the summer. In fact, who could ask for anything more, Jim had thought.

Julie had earned her master's degree at the same school Jim had, and it was only natural that she would return to Utah to get her doctorate where her dad taught. Julie had long blond hair and brown eyes, stood about five feet eight inches tall, and had a beautiful smile to match her eyes. Always being the outdoor type, simply because of her dad's work at the college, she became interested in archaeology as a young student in high school, particularly after helping her dad find the remains of an Indian burial site in the Carbon County area of Utah. From that point on, she was hooked on it and went after it with gusto, learning all she could about the ancient inhabitants of Carbon, Emery, and Sevier Counties. Her mom had passed away from cervical cancer when she was only fourteen years old, that was the hardest part of her life. Her father, in order to deal with the loss of his wife, just went deeper into his work as an archeologist. In order to remain close with her dad, Julie went with him on all of his digs. This had created a time of healing for both of them and a greater bond between them.

Jim was a young man with many talents. Being more of a bookworm, he became fascinated with the wild west and the legends of Wyatt Earp, Doc Holliday, Bat Masterson, and Billy the kid while reading about them. When he started reading about Geronimo, Sitting Bull, and Cochise, his interest turned to the Indians and their way of life and their later hardships of adapting to the white man's ways of living. As he continued studying the old Indian ways, he found an interest there that couldn't be quenched by just reading anymore. Enrolling in college and moving through the undergraduate and graduate programs, he was surprised by how much he didn't know about the American Indian and how powerful the Indian nations were at one time.

Following his love, Julie, to Utah, he found what he was looking for at BYU when it came to learning more about the American Indian and their predecessors. Taking field trips to the San Rafael Swell and Nine Mile Canyon to look at the Indian rock paintings just made Jim want to learn more about all of the Indians, such as the Nez Perce, Anasazi, Ute, and the Fremont Indian cultures, that had lived and migrated throughout Utah and the surrounding states.

Being in the Royal Gorge area of Colorado, the idea was to find out more about the Ute Indian tribe that had been in the area for many years and to study their habitats and their way of life in the canyon. Spending most of their time examining the artifacts at the existing dig, the trio decided to take a break and go exploring on the south side of the park the following day.

Driving the Professor's jeep across the gorge onto the south side of the park, they started looking for any signs of habitation by the Ute Indian tribe. Starting from the north end of the park, they drove across the Royal Gorge bridge through the southern area that had been burned a few years back by a forest fire. Although it had been several years since the fire, the ground vegetation was just now starting to regrow, making it easier to explore the south side of the gorge as they looked for artifacts dealing with the Ute Indians and where they had lived.

Not finding any indication of the Utes' having lived in this portion of the park, they continued going deeper into the canyon to the more rugged part of the mountains where the canyons started forming. They looked for any small caves where mounds were found at the entrance of the cave, this indicated the garbage that had been left behind by the Indians as they migrated to and from their camping sites. They were also hoping to find caches where the Indians would store food near the rock outcroppings for future use as they traveled through the canyon. The Utes were a nomadic mountain tribe who would follow their source of food throughout the year all across Colorado, Utah, New Mexico, and parts of Wyoming, as their sources of food migrated from place to place. During the summer they would head high into the Rocky Mountains, the Wasatch Mountains, and the Uintah Mountains and then go into the lowlands onto the plains during the wintertime, killing the bison, deer, and fishing as needed to survive the winter cold. The belief of the Utes was that everything had a purpose and was not to be taken for granted or misused in any way. The Great Spirit was there to protect everything that lived, and that included them being promised that they would conquer their enemies in battle and never be separated as a nation.

After stopping the jeep they got out and made their way to the top of the cliffs and started looking down into the steep canyons. Jim, on his second sweep of the area, spotted a cave opening on the face of one of the cliffs. He pointed it out to the others. He grabbed his binoculars and was able to see a mound in the front of the opening.

"I see a mound in the front of the cave; we need to go check it out," Jim said excitedly.

Looking at the terrain surrounding the cave, they moved the jeep to the other side just above the cave, so they could use it as an anchor for the rope.

"I'll go get the rope; I think you're going to need it," Dr. Wainwright said.

After anchoring the rope to the jeep, and throwing it over the side of the cliff, Jim put on a harness and slowly lowered himself down to the entrance to the cave. Not seeing anything out of the ordinary, he used his flashlight to peer inside. All at once a flash went by him startling him, almost causing him to drop his light. Julie and Dr. Wainwright could hear him yell out. Looking down into the cliff face and seeing him hanging by the rope, Julie yelled out, "Are you all right, what happened?"

By now Jim had gotten himself righted again and called back up to the top, "Stupid owl just spooked me!"

Upon hearing this Julie started to laugh. "Watch out for flying mice down there too."

"Really funny, really funny!"

At this point Jim kept looking inside the cave with his light. The cave was big enough that Jim could crawl into it and rest on the ledge. Looking deeper into the cave, he saw that it went for about three feet and then ended. Searching the walls of the cave, he looked for any evidence of Indian artwork, seeing none he leaned over the edge of the cliff, looking for other signs outside the cave. As he sat there he started to go through the mound, finding bits and pieces of bone and pottery fragments that were left behind by the Ute Indians. He gathered what he could and put it into his backpack to look at later when he was back at camp. As he was gathering the stuff up, he noticed something shiny in the dirt. Picking it up and looking at it, he realized it was a medallion of some sort that he had never seen before. The medallion was about two inches tall and an inch wide with beads of rock in the center of it. The rock was clear quartz with purple crystals in the ring around the clear quartz. Shoving the medallion into his shirt pocket for safe keeping, he shone the light back into the cave again, this time being slower in moving the flashlight around inside the cave. As he looked into the back of the cave, he realized there was a 90-degree turn at the wall that made it look as if the cave was shallow. Off to the side was another part of the wall that laid a little further back. This time, crawling towards the back of the cave, he found that the opening went deeper, and it opened into a bigger room. Taking his rope off, he stood up inside the cave, and using his flashlight he began walking around. This time the Indian artwork was there and so was the pottery that hadn't been broken yet and other artifacts as well. As he searched the cave, he came across a skull and some bones lying on the ground next to the wall of the cave. Taking his camera out, he started taking pictures of everything inside the cave. After about a half hour of exploring, he headed back out to the front of the cave, reattached himself to the rope, and crawled back up the face of the cliff to join Julie and Dr. Wainwright. Being excited, he showed the medallion to both of them, "We've found a cave that no one has seen or knows about!"

Describing what he saw in there, i.e., the bones of the Indian and the artwork on the cave walls, it took Jim twenty minutes to get over being excited. The rest of the day was spent with all three of them going back into the cave and seeing for themselves what Jim had described to them. When Julie and Dr. Wainwright saw what Jim had described, they realized it was even better than what they had expected to see. The hard part was using the ropes to get from the face of the cave back to the top of the cliff as they made their different trips up and down the rope. Having only one basket to put the artifacts in made it easier at this point for whoever who was on top of the cliff to pull it up. Dr. Wainwright decided to stay on top of the cliff for this part of the operation, mainly due to his age.

The only question that was on the doctor's mind was, why was this cave even here and how did the Indians access the cave themselves, seeing as how it was on the face of a cliff. Seeing no rope inside the cave and only pottery inside, the question continued to linger in the back of the doctor's mind. By now it was getting dark and they needed to head back to their campsite, where their equipment was, and their camp was set up for sleeping. Taking what they could carry, they left the cave for the next day. They spent most of the night checking out everything that they brought back with them. The one piece that everybody was wondering about was the medallion. What did it mean, why was it there, and who wore it?

Getting to bed late that night, the three of them were up early the next morning, excited about going back to the cave. In fact, it was all they could do to eat breakfast and pack lunches for the afternoon. Setting off again to head back to the cave, they took off, wasting no time to get there. By nine o'clock they were getting the ropes out and harnessing themselves to the ropes to go back down into the cave. In their preparations, they brought some big baskets with them to hold more artifacts and stuff, if needed.

Jim was the first to go back down to make sure everything was as safe as it was yesterday. Julie came next. Dr. Wainwright, being older, would stay topside and haul the baskets up as needed so that he could study and categorize what they found in the cave. Jim had brought some portable lights that would allow the two of them to see more clearly inside the cave. This really made a difference once they were turned on. The cave was bigger than they had originally thought. There was another room, although smaller, that was further back into the mountain. Julie focused her attention looking in the main room while Jim went into the smaller room to look around. Taking one of the stationary lights with him, he set it up inside the smaller room to see what was in there. The floor of the room was covered in about three inches of dust that had accumulated over the years. As Jim sifted through the dust, he found bits of bone and pottery. In his search he was able to find remnants of a bedroll made of woven cloth and bowls that were still in one piece and also some pottery shards. He called out to Julie, "Come see what I found in this other room."

Julie came in and looked at everything in the room. "It looks as if it had been the sleeping quarters for whoever the skeleton was."

"I agree, take a look at the walls in here. It looks as if the paintings tell a story about something that happened years ago."

"Yes, you're right, but what does it say? I've never seen these kinds of figures used before in these kind of paintings," Julie said as she pointed them out to Jim.

"It looks as if it's telling a story about a battle that occurred between two men. You can see one of the men lying down while the other has a knife in his hands."

"Yeah, you're right. Let me get some pictures of this. Maybe your dad has seen them before."

Julie returned to her part of the cave and continued working in the old fireplace in the center of the cave. Jim started taking pictures inside the room and identifying the locations of everything in the smaller room.

As Jim continued to go through the smaller room, he found a small bag under the bedroll; opening it, he found a coin inside the bag. Shining his flashlight onto the coin, he could tell it was a Spanish coin. On one side of the coin was a cross with writing on the outside and with figures of animals in the center. The other side of the coin had what appeared to be two palm trees standing over a river. Jim looked through the bag and didn't find anything else. Going back over to where he found the coin bag, he sifted through the dust again and found a rolled parchment. Carefully putting it inside his back pack to protect it, he came out of the smaller room and showed the coin to Julie.

Julie's eyes lit up, thinking of buried treasure and being rich, but when Jim said that he had only found one coin and the parchment, you could see the disappointment in her eyes that came just as quick. Still, the idea of finding a gold coin was exciting. For the rest of the day they worked on the cave, referencing and categorizing everything they found inside it.

One of the laws of the land was that the burial site of the body was not to be moved or removed from its resting place, unless you were willing to pay a fine to the BLM (Bureau of Land Management). This was done to keep amateur archeologists from stealing the artifacts and selling them on the black market. The real archeologist could go in and document everything but could not desecrate the site in any way. That being said, the work of finding out what was in the jars of pottery now started and the other things that were found were slowly being checked against other data that had been collected from other sites throughout the years. Once the work was complete, the responsibility of the discoverers was to report the location and what was found in the cave to the Indian tribe council to let them know that it had been found, and all the data put together on the site would be given to the council for their records as well.

After closing out the site, the artifacts they took to evaluate were taken back to the base camp to be reviewed, cleaned up, and recorded and then returned to the cave as well. Once all this was completed and everything was returned, then for all practical purposes, the cave would be returned to its previous state, as if no one had ever been there.

Chapter III

With everything gathered from the cave and brought back to the base camp, the real work now began in identifying all the artifacts that had been found, cross-referencing them to what had already been found in other locations. These would be cataloged as coming from a new site and a new location. The work would be documented in the proper journals used by the colleges and universities, showing what had been found that was different from previous locations in the same area and other areas where the Ute Indians had also lived. A ton of work was just starting for the three of them. The finding was the fun part; the hard part would be the rest of the organizing, cataloging, and documenting everything that they had found.

All three decided to stay at the base camp for the rest of their time simply because it would take some time to review everything that had been collected and cleaned up, especially the parchment. The Professor would work on this himself, simply because he had the experience of doing this before on other digs he had been on.

Jim and Julie would once again be the students watching and learning from the teacher. The Professor was patient in his explanation of dealing with the parchment. While he worked on the outer parts of the parchment container, knowing this was going to take some time, he suggested to Jim and Julie, "Why don't you guys clean up the other pieces that we found at the site. I'll let you know when I'm ready to show you more of what I'm doing."

Jim and Julie agreed with the Professor and started to work on cleaning up the other artifacts that had been collected. Separating the artifacts between the two of them, they had one basket they were drawing the artifacts from, and the other basket was used for the cleaned-up pieces to be put in. Again, each piece had to be identified and marked with a number after it had been accounted for in a book binder. Julie would put it down in the binder while Jim would clean the artifact, and between the two of them they would identify it.

Sorting everything out went on for hours, and by nightfall the Professor was ready to start working on the parchment. Dissecting the cloth around the parchment was laborious, simply because of the age of the material and how brittle the parchment was inside the cloth. Being able to get the cloth off the parchment was a major undertaking in and of itself. Jim and Julie, when finished with their part of the job, sat and watched the Professor do his thing as he worked the cloth off the parchment. Under normal circumstances, none of this would be done out in the field. This would be done in a controlled environment in a clean room with x-ray equipment standing by. However, due to having no colleges nearby with the right kind of equipment, except in Colorado Springs, this would have to do.

With the parchment still rolled up and lying on top of the table, the Professor proceeded to move forward in opening it. Overall, the parchment was in good condition, and once the Professor had it opened they found a piece of rolled leather inside it. Peeling away the parchment from the leather, they were able to unroll the leather. Jim was standing by with a camera to take pictures of what they found on the leather. Carefully unrolling the leather, a picture appeared on the leather, showing in the lower right-hand corner a river drawn by two wavy lines, and in the middle of the leather was a group of mountains, with the one on the front being shaped like a human skull. There on the front of the skull was a hole, marking a cave with the symbol of a medicine man in front of it. The upper right and left sections of the leather were shown to have a picture of a canyon, having a mountain range with a skull in the center of the canyon. There were some symbols along the bottom of the mountains and also above the canyon on the leather that were partially destroyed and were unable to be identified.

As all three of them looked at the leather, Julie said, "It looks like a map to a cave somewhere."

"It is a map," Jim said.

"Do you two remember an old Indian legend about a cave being watched over by the tribe's medicine man?" the Professor asked.

"In fact, I do remember something about a cave being cursed to keep others out of it," Jim said.

"Do you think this is a map to the cave?" Julie asked.

"It could be," the Professor said.

"Well, what do we do now?" Julie asked.

"Jim, do you still have that medallion you found at the entrance to the cave?" asked the Professor.

Jim had forgotten all about it until the Professor mentioned it. Pulling it from his shirt pocket, he showed it to the Professor. "I haven't had a chance to clean it up yet."

As the Professor looked at the medallion, he placed it on the map next to the writing on the top of the leather and then down to the bottom of the leather. At first glance, you couldn't see any resemblance in the medallion next to the symbols on the leather. Jim caught sight of it first, pointing it out to the other two as they looked at the map and medallion. "Look at the edges on the top and bottom of the medallion."

After studying the medallion Julie pointed out, "The medallion is a map as well, resembling the leather map."

Jim was the next to see the comparison of the medallion and the map. "I guess the medicine man kept the medallion around his neck so that the map could be kept safe and buried somewhere else."

"I believe you're right on that, Jim," the Professor said.

Jim took the medallion and, taking some water and alcohol, cleaned it up so they could get a better idea of what it looked like. Julie took some twine and gave it to Jim to make a necklace from it with the medallion hanging on it. Jim put the medallion around his neck and went back to looking at the leather map. By now it was too late to scout the areas depicted on the map, so they put everything back together. They carefully rolled the leather map, putting it back into the parchment paper and the cloth, then put it all in a plastic bag and finally into a metal container for safekeeping.

The rest of the night was for preparing dinner and getting ready for bed. Jim slept in his own tent as did Julie and her father. As they sat watching the fire, letting it burn itself out, they all watched the coals of the fire glowing till there was nothing left. All turning in for the night, they crawled into their sleeping bags and turned off the lanterns. All was quiet for the evening. The stars were bright, and the Milky Way could be seen in the night sky. Lying near the river, they could hear it as it moved along through the canyon. The river at night had a lulling effect on everybody, and pretty soon all was quiet in the camp as everybody was asleep.

During the night Jim had a dream of seeing a medicine man standing and looking at him and, using his hands, he kept showing a way to the mountains behind him. The medicine man would start walking in the direction of the mountains and then stop and motion for Jim to follow. As Jim got up in his dream, he followed the medicine man on a trail that was clearly marked, and as they walked the medicine man would point things out to him. Jim was trying to take all of this in, but it was very frustrating due to the fact he had no idea of where he was. At one point the medicine man stopped and waited for Jim, pointing to him and then to a mountain, then disappeared.

Jim woke up with a start, and as he lay there he was trying to remember everything he had seen in his dream, trying to determine if it was just a bad dream or whatever it could be, all the while trying to make sense of it. Not knowing what to think, he finally went back to sleep. Again, the medicine man came to him in his dreams. This time the medicine man was fighting with someone and was wounded in the battle. Gathering all his strength, the medicine man killed his opponent with his knife. The medicine man, knowing he was mortally wounded, half walking and half dragging himself, went back to his cave using a trail only he knew about. He went into the cave and taking the wrapped casing with the leather map in it, put it under his blanket before lying down in the big portion of the cave. In a matter of hours he died. As he lay there waiting to die, he sang the warrior song he had grown up with, hoping the Great Spirit would be proud of him for giving his life to keep the cave safe from the unbelievers and forgive him for dying without having someone to pass on the duties of the medicine man to protect the cave.

This time Jim was a little slower coming out of the dream, and as he did, he realized that the first dream was for him to know where to look for the treasure. The second dream was to make sure that he understood his part in it. He would be the protector of the cave, as if chosen by the medicine man. Not being so alarmed by the second dream, he knew that his mission in life was to safeguard the cave. This time as he went to sleep, he was brought into another dream. The medicine man, coming to him once more, placed the medallion on his neck and smiled. The medicine man, looking towards heaven, spoke in his dialect, "I have completed my mission," and looking at Jim, he continued, "It is now yours to start."

Jim knew that the language of the medicine man was speaking was his own language, but Jim understood what he had said. Jim raised his hands in the dream and said, "Great Spirit, give me the strength to carry out my duties."

At that point, lightning flashed across the sky, and as he stood there he watched the medicine man, now dressed in a full headdress with a tomahawk in one hand and an obsidian-bladed knife in the other hand, reach into the sky with both hands extended and melt into the clouds above him. As he did so, the clouds took him up, and as he disappeared into the clouds, Jim watched until the clouds disappeared as well. A voice was heard from the clouds that only Jim would understand: "As long as you are worthy of this calling, you will be protected from your enemies."

Jim nodded his head in understanding and, looking towards the sky with his own hands raised to the sky, bowed his head in agreement. As the lightning flashed once more from the heavens, this time it hit the medallion, thus energizing not only the medallion but Jim as well. Jim then gave a sign that the medicine man understood. "I will go and do and be as you have asked."

Jim was completely wide awake now and any thoughts of going back to sleep were gone. He was now ready for the day to begin. The sun was just starting to show over the mountains, and as it chased the shadows across the valley and the mountains, they tried to hide from the sunlight. Jim sat and watched all of this, now realizing and understanding what he had agreed to. He now began to prepare himself for the next journey in his life which now lay before him, not knowing what the future held for him and wondering why he had been chosen by the old medicine man.

Looking around the campsite and listening to the river as it flowed through the canyon, Jim imagined what it must have been like hundreds of years ago, living as an Indian and being responsible for the most sacred knowledge of what lay in the cave, yet to be discovered by him and the others.

Chapter IV

Jim sat by the campfire that he had just built and began to warm up from the morning chill. A little later he decided to start cooking some breakfast for the others. The smell of the bacon and eggs woke the other two up, and as they moved closer to the fire to warm up, Jim handed them the food he had prepared for them. Sitting there eating and not saying a word, Jim smiled. "Boy, you two are not morning people at all, are you?"

Julie was the first to answer. "Morning people make me mad, so happy, cheerful, and singing. It's enough to make you want to crawl back into bed."

The Professor sat there and looked at each of them, smiling. "Don't look at me; she gets it from her mother's side of the family."

Jim laughed. "The things you learn about your intended on your first camping trip."

Julie tried to smile but it didn't come off well. She just sat there eating her breakfast, not saying another word. Jim was lost in thought as he pondered on what last night's dreams meant as he ate his breakfast. He was trying to decide whether or not to tell Julie or the Professor about his dreams and was wondering where to start looking for the cave.

As he thought about this question, he was looking into the flames of the fire, once again deep in thought. Julie stood up and came over and sat down next to him. "A penny for your thoughts."

This startled Jim to the point of him almost falling into the fire. Julie caught him by his belt before he fell forward. "I'm sorry, I didn't mean to scare you like that."

"I'm sorry too. I didn't hear you sit down next to me."

Julie looked at him for the first time. "Are you all right? You don't look so good; did you get enough sleep last night?"

Jim looked at her. "Yes, I'm fine, I look like this every morning, and no, I didn't sleep well last night."

Julie was surprised by his answer. "What happened? How come you didn't sleep good?"

"I'll tell you later...when the time is right."

By now Jim was getting up and moving to gather up some of his gear and a canteen full of water. "Professor, I'm going out for a hike this morning. If you need me, I should be back by lunch time."

Both the Professor and Julie just sat there, not knowing what to say, as Jim headed off down the canyon, following the trail. Julie wondered if she had said something wrong to upset him. Looking at her father, he gave her a hug. "He'll be all right; just be patient with him."

Jim walked on down the trail next to the river, looking for the sights he had seen in his dreams. Not knowing what direction to go, he kept following the river. Pausing for just a moment, he sat down on a rock to catch his breath. As he sat there, he saw a trail that seemed to go up into the mountain. He remembered this trail from his dream and started to follow it into the mountain. Walking for almost two hours uphill, he saw the mountain from the dream he had in front of him, further up the trail. He continued to follow the trail as he made his way towards the mountain. As he continued to follow the trail, it became steeper and more of a challenge to climb. Resting more often now than usual, he eventually made his way to the mountain. Standing there on the trail, he noticed that the trail split in two different directions at the top; now the question was which trail to follow. The trail on the left would take him into a small canyon; the trail to the right continued going deeper into the mountain. Sitting down and thinking, trying to remember the dream, he didn't remembered seeing the trail split like this. Not knowing which way to go and now realizing it was close to noon, he looked at his watch and, seeing it was eleven thirty already, decided he'd better go back to camp. Thinking it would have to be another day to choose which trail to follow, Jim headed back to camp before the Professor or Julie started to worry about him.

"At least I know the way to the mountain now, and it isn't just my imagination," he said, talking to himself.

Arriving back in camp at about one o'clock, Julie came running up to him and, putting her arms around him, just held him for a moment. "We were about to send out a search party for you, if you hadn't showed up when you did."

The Professor came walking up to them and, seeing Jim, was relieved that he was all right. "You had us worried being gone for so long, Jim. Is everything all right?"

"Yes, sir, I just went farther than I had planned to go, and I didn't realize how long I'd been gone until I looked at my watch."

Julie was still holding him as they walked back to the camp and sat down in one of the chairs under the shade cover. Julie brought him some water to drink and made sure he had everything that he needed. Jim smiled at her. "Your morning charm is made up by your afternoon charm."

Julie smiled and hit him in the shoulder. "Next time, we all go with you."

Jim nodded his head in agreement and kept drinking his water from the cup. By now everything was back to normal. Julie and Jim continued working on the other artifacts that had been found near where they were camped. The Professor was busy reading his reference books about some of the artifacts that lay before him. One page he was reading had a picture of an Indian wearing the same medallion around his neck that Jim now had with him. The Professor got up and brought the book over to Jim and Julie. "Hey Jim, take a look at this."

Jim, taking the book, studied the picture and he saw the medallion on the Indian's neck. "It's the same medallion that I found!"

Julie leaned over to look at the picture as well, nodding her head in agreement. "Does it say which tribe he belongs to or what it means?"

"No, it doesn't, except from my understanding only the medicine man was allowed to wear the medallion," said Jim, looking at the picture.

"How do you know that?" asked Julie.

"According to the legend, there was only one person who could wear the medallion, and it was always the medicine man who wore it," replied Jim.

The Professor, shaking his head in agreement, said, "Jim is right about that," then adding, "I didn't know you knew so much about the legend, Jim!"

"You might say I've had a crash course on it over the last couple of days."

"Well, that's good, I think. By the way, not to change the subject, but I need to go to town and send in my report and the pictures we've taken to the university. Is there anything either of you need me to pick up while I'm in town?"

Jim and Julie both shook their heads no as the Professor got himself ready for the trip. In a few minutes the Professor got into the Jeep and started the engine and waved goodbye. "I should be back in about an hour or two at the most; try not to miss me."

"Drive carefully, Dad. We'll have dinner ready when you get back," Julie said.

As the two of them watched the Professor leave in the Jeep, they looked at each other, trying to decide what to do till the Professor got back. As Jim sat down under the shade of the tarp, he decided to tell Julie about the dreams that he had had the night before. "Julie, I need to tell you something about last night and why I went for the hike today."

"Should I sit down for this?"

"You'd better, because you won't believe what I've got to tell you."

Sitting down in the shade and waiting to hear what Jim had to say, Julie waited patiently for him to start. After a couple of seconds of trying to figure where to start, Jim found the words and began to explain what had happened the night before with the two dreams he had about the medicine man in the cave.

"I had two dreams last night, both dealing with the medicine man from the cave. Then I had a third dream about the medallion." He then continued to explain what he had learned about the medallion. "The medicine man told me it was now my responsibility to keep the cave secure and safe. He was the last of his tribe chosen to protect and take care of the cave. Now he's turned the responsibility over to me."

When he finished telling her what he'd learned from his dreams, he sat there waiting for Julie's reply. After a couple of minutes of letting what he had said to Julie sink in, he asked her, "Well, what do you think about what I've told you?"

She sat there for a minute, looking down at the ground without saying anything. Finally, she looked up at him, "First of all, I believe you; the reason is that I've had some dreams as well about the medicine man we found in the cave."

He looked at Julie, surprised that she believed him, but also that she had had a dream as well about the medicine man. Looking dumbfounded, he asked, "What were your dreams about? What did he show you?"

"He did share the same things you saw, but he also told me about the medallion you have and how it has become your mission in life to be the new protector for the cave. He also told me how important it is for you to live up to the responsibilities of being the guardian of the cave."

Jim looked relieved that Julie had seen the same things in her dream as well. "I thought you might think I was going crazy after I told you about my dreams."

"The medicine man told me that I needed to help you to find the cave and make sure that no one else knew about it. He also warned me that there would be others who would try to take away the medallion from you in order to find the cave and steal what was in it."

"Well, I think I've found the mountain where the cave is that I saw in my dreams."

"Was that the reason for the hike this morning?"

"Yes, I wanted to make sure it wasn't just a dream that I had. I found a trail that leads to one of the mountains I saw in my dreams. The problem is that the trail I took splits into two trails about two miles up from the river. One part of the trail leads away from the mountain I saw in my dreams and into a canyon, and the other one goes deeper into the mountain."

"You found the trail and the mountain?"

"Yes, I did. The problem is that the mountain in the dream might just be a marker and not the direction I need to go to find the cave."

"Do you remember at what angle you saw the mountain in your dream?"

Jim thought for a moment. "The medicine man pointed it out to me on his left side; in other words, he was taking the trail that went straight. How could I have been so blind not to see this before?"

"That's why you have me, kiddo, to tell you where to go once in a while," Julie said, laughing.

"Ha, ha, ha, you keep that up and I might just marry you yet."

As they sat and visited with each other, Jim decided to ask Julie about her dreams. "Please tell me more about your dreams."

"There isn't much more to tell, except that I was to be with you in your quest to find the cave. The one thing that stood out was that there would be others who would be interested in getting the medallion away from you and would do anything to get it. The impression I had was that it would be hard to keep the ones who wanted it away from you."

"In my dream, the medicine man killed one of the men who was trying to take the medallion away from him. I hope I don't have to do that in order to protect the cave."

"Me too. It would be terrible if you had to do that."

As they both thought about the dreams each of them had, both of them realized that this was a serious mission they were undertaking. Julie asked, "Why us, why not somebody else, and why now, and who could want what was in the cave enough to kill us for it?"

"I think it has to do with the fact that we found the cave and the medallion. We were the first people in the cave after so many years of it being lost and forgotten about. I believe we were chosen not only because of who we are but because we would know that it had to be protected from the others who would try to make money off of what they found in the cave."

"So, what are you planning on doing the rest of your life now that you have the medallion in your possession?"

"Actually, it's more like what are we planning to do with the rest of our lives now that we have the medallion in our possession?"

Both Jim and Julie looked at each other, realizing that finding the cave now would have consequences that neither of them could fathom. The medicine man was right in choosing them to be the guardians of the cave. Between the two of them, they would watch and wait, being ready for the unknown to prove the medicine man right. The challenge for both of them was to expect the unexpected from wherever it came and to be ready for it. This mission had become their mission as well as the Professors', unbeknownst to him. All three of them together would protect the cave from the unseen threats that would come to be.

Waiting for the Professor to return from town, both Julie and Jim could hardly wait to tell him about their dreams and the responsibility that now fell on all three of them. While they waited for the Professor to return, Julie decided to prepare their evening meal. Jim, not wanting to look at any of the other artifacts, decided to take a walk down to the river and spend some time contemplating the events of the day. After a few minutes he made his way back to camp to help Julie with dinner.

Chapter V

The Professor arrived back at camp, getting there just a little after six o'clock. Julie, as promised, had dinner cooking when he returned, and she was busy with all the food preparation, cooking over the open fire. Jim stood by the campfire to help as Julie might need.

"So how was your trip to the big city?" Julie asked, as she looked up from the fire.

"The trip was uneventful and actually a nice drive to and from the city. You know, I've been thinking about what we have found out here, and I'm concerned there may be some fallout from others who want to know more about what we have found."

"What do you mean Professor?" Jim asked.

"Normally, if you find something of worth or value as a Professor, you want to share it with the world. Well, I'm not sure, but we might have found something that should have remained lost for the good of all concerned. The way I see it, only time will tell now that I've told the world about the cave and the skeleton inside it."

Jim, looking at Julie, smiled. "Have we got a tale for you to hear, Professor."

For the rest of the evening Jim and Julie related their experiences from the dreams they had the night before and how Jim found one of the mountains from his dreams on his hike and the trail he took to find it. The Professor listened intently as each told of their dreams, trying to decide what to do with the new information he now had. After each of them was finished with describing their dreams, he looked at both of them for a second. "Do you know what this entails for the both of you and now me? We need to find the cave as soon as we can and determine what is in the cave to decide whether to close it for good or share what we have found with the rest of the world."

"I guess it depends on what we find inside it, don't you think, Professor?" Jim asked.

"Yes, yes, of course it does. But if it's like the part of the Book of Mormon that has been hidden, maybe it's time now for it to come forth."

"Is it really our call for us to decide?" Julie asked.

"I don't know; I guess it all depends on what we find in the cave. If it's riches like gold, I say we seal it up and forget about it. If it's records, then it becomes another situation of do we translate the records for the rest of the world or do we lock them up out of sight and save them for another day?"

As they stood there thinking about what the Professor said, he continued, "Either way, we need to find the cave before we have others coming to search for it who are less interested in the historical value of what they might find and more interested in the value of what the cave might have in it."

"I suggest we start tomorrow after an early breakfast to find the cave. The way I see it, we only have a few days before the world will beat a path here to find it for themselves," Jim said.

"It's too bad it's so late tonight; we could leave now to go find it," Julie said.

"Tomorrow will be soon enough to begin our search for it," the Professor said.

The rest of the night was spent on getting food and stuff ready that they would need to start tomorrow morning on their hike. By midnight all were in their sleeping bags fast asleep, ready for the hike of their lifetimes the following day.

The next morning all were awake at sunrise. Breakfast was prepared and eaten by the time the sun was coming up over the mountains. Each of them was carrying a canteen full of water and ready with their hiking boots on and carrying a backpack with their lunches, extra pair of socks, pants, and shirts inside, along with their cameras and snacks to eat along the trail. Each of them was wearing a hat to protect them from the sun and had a bandanna on, just in case some emergency occurred along the trail. Jim carried a fifty-foot rope, just in case they had to climb or rappel to find the cave. All in all, they were prepared for the most obvious of circumstances they might encounter along the way on the trail.

Jim took the lead, as he already knew where to go to find the cave. The easy part was finding the trail which led from the river. From there it was uphill and again they stopped as needed for everybody to catch their breath as they made their way up to the fork in the trail. Jim stopped at this point. "This is where I turned around because I didn't know which trail to take from here. Julie provided the insight I needed to know which trail to take. We will stay on the trail that leads us away from the mountain, as indicated in my dream."

As they continued following the trail, they found they were getting into some pine trees and leaving the buck brush behind. Stopping under one of the pines where the shade was, Jim kept looking at his surroundings to verify what he had seen in his dreams. As the other two sat in the shade, Jim decided to move up the trail a little way to get his bearings. Standing there within eyesight of the other two, he continued looking all around the area. He then sat down on the ground to catch his breath as well, and he could see another mountain from the angle below the pine tree he was seated next to.

As he sat there, he took out his canteen, and as he was drinking from it, the angle of the mountain across the canyon caught his eye. Putting the canteen down, he kept looking at the mountain and then stood up, saying to the others, "We are on the right trail; I recognize the mountain over there from my dream."

After resting for another five minutes, they got up and continued following the trail, still climbing towards the top of the mountain. Within an hour they had reached the summit. The trail was now headed across the ridge line. They headed towards the other side of the ridge, where there was a cliff that was jutting out over the canyon below it. The trail had gotten a little harder to follow as they made their way to the face of the cliff. In some places the trail disappeared into the rock outcroppings. Jim would go further out past the rocky areas and find the trail once more, then come back to get the other two to show them the way.

By midday they had made it to the other side of the cliff face and, finding some shade under a big rock, they decided to have some lunch there. Jim laid back on the rope he was carrying and dozed while Julie assisted her dad with his backpack to make it more comfortable for him to carry. Jim woke up about thirty minutes later. "Are you ready to continue?"

This time, both Julie and her dad looked at him with a look of dread on their faces. They stood up again, a little slower this time, feeling a little sore, as if knowing that the trail was only going to get harder as they continued to go on. Jim, sensing this, said, "I've got a feeling it isn't much further for us to go now."

"For all of our sakes, I hope you're right about this," the Professor said, as he took one long drink from his canteen before putting it back on his shoulder.

Jim could tell both of them were spent and there wasn't anything he could do to help in any way to ease the loads they were carrying. He was hoping he was right about being close to the cave. Following the trail for another hundred yards, the trail disappeared again. As Julie and the Professor waited, Jim walked up a little further, hoping he would find the trail once again. But this time he came back with a puzzled look on his face. "I can't find the trail; I believe this is the end of the trail for us to follow."

"Then that must mean we are here, near the cave," Julie said, as she started looking around the area.

Now the Professor was looking around as well, hoping he would see the cave somewhere out there. Jim kept studying the area where the trail disappeared, walking up and down towards the face of the cliff. Looking at the face of the cliff, he saw what looked like a small indentation in the rock. Pointing it out to the other two, half walking, half crawling, he headed towards the face of the cliff where the indentation was, and as he got closer he thought it was a small opening that led into the mountain. It was about the same size as the first cave where they found the remains of the medicine man. Getting closer to the face of the cliff, Jim finally was able to see that the opening in the rock was nothing more than a few missing rocks where the shade rested. As he stood there looking around, he was trying to remember his dream about the location of the cave. Then he yelled to the other two, "Nothing down here."

Jim slowly started making his way back up to where Julie and the Professor were on the top of the ridge. Crawling up the mountain on the loose rock was frustrating because as he would crawl up two feet at a time he would slide back down one foot. He was feeling the effects of the hike now in his legs and was wishing that there was an easier way to get back to Julie and the Professor.

Julie and her dad, who were disappointed in what Jim had said, now started looking all around the area. It was Julie who saw a shaded area behind a group of trees further up the mountain. "Look over there in the trees."

Pointing it out to her father, they both started hiking up to the trees. Jim saw from his vantage point that Julie was moving towards the trees and watched as the two of them moved away from the face of the cliff, further up the mountain. Finally making his way back to where he started, he rested while Julie and the Professor worked their way to the group of trees. Waiting to hear from Julie and the Professor, he slowly got up to follow them.

When he got to the trees where he thought he saw Julie and the Professor the last time, he waited for them. They were not anywhere to be found, it was as if they had disappeared into the trees. Jim started getting worried now and started looking around, calling their names out loud. In a few minutes Julie reappeared. "Jim, you need to see this."

Taking Jim by the hand, she led him into the clump of trees. As they walked into the trees, it was only then that the cave appeared to him. Julie smiled as she watched Jim as he realized what he was looking at. He looked at her excitedly. By now Julie was nodding her head in agreement to Jim's questioning eyes. Taking him by the hand, she led him into the cave. As they walked in, they saw the Professor sitting on a rock in the center of the cave, looking at a table with gold plates everywhere, along with other things like gold cups, plates to eat on, facemasks and headdresses. As Jim was looking around, he also saw small figurines of animals made from gold and gold artwork hanging on the walls of the cave. Everywhere he looked, all he could see was gold. There were even Spanish helmets that the conquistadors had worn located in the cave. There was a light on that showed the full size of the cave, but the light wasn't coming from anything that they had carried with them into the cave; it just seemed to emanate from somewhere within the cave. Jim just stood there mesmerized by what he was looking at. Julie, taking him by the hand again, led him to where the Professor was seated and showed him the golden plates that had writing on them, along with a Spanish sword sitting on the table next to the plates. There were gold plates everywhere on the floor of the cave. Some were stacked on top of each other, and some of the stacks of plates were as high as the ceiling of the cave, others were lying on the ground by themselves. In one corner of the cave was a pile of gold coins, just sitting there on the ground with chest armor nearby it. Julie picked up one of the coins. "Do you think the Spanish are going to miss their gold?"

The Professor looked up at Jim and smiled. "I believe we found the cave the medicine man told you about."

Jim was speechless, still trying to take it all in. In fact, all he could do was touch the plates and smile. For Jim, he had never seen anything like this before, except maybe from the pictures taken in the tombs of Egypt, where they found the burial places of the pharaohs. He sat down next to the plates and started reading them to see if he could make sense of any of it. The writing was from an ancient Judeo text that he didn't understand. The writing was more symbolic than letters. Looking at the Professor, he answered, "I can't read it, either; this is a new language that I've never seen before."

Jim kept looking at the plates, wishing he had paid more attention in the ancient-language classes that he had attended. Julie walked over to where Jim and her father were sitting and, looking at them, asked, "What do we do now that we know where it is?"

"We keep it hidden from the world, that's what we do. How we do that is simple; we pretend we never found it."

The Professor, listening to Jim, said, "I think we need to confirm what we found but do it in a way that nobody knows that we found it in this cave. So, do you think it would be all right to take some of these plates back with us to BYU and have them looked at for translation?"

Jim thought to himself, knowing the promise he made to the medicine man in his dream. He also thought that it would be fascinating to find out if anyone could actually decipher the symbols on the plates. "I don't know if it would be allowed by the medicine man," he said looking at the Professor.

While they sat there discussing the situation, the medicine man showed himself to Jim and Julie once again. Jim and Julie stood there trying to understand what he was saying to them. The medicine man reached down and picked up one of the plates lying on the floor of the cave, handing it to Jim and motioning with his other hand, saying to go in peace. The Professor, not seeing anything except Jim and Julie staring off into the back of the cave and Jim having the plate in his hand, was wondering what they were staring at.

"What's wrong; what are you staring at?" he asked Jim.

Jim turned to him, "We have permission to take this plate with us back to BYU."

"You didn't see him, Father, the medicine man?" Julie asked.

"See what? I didn't see anything at all."

Jim and Julie looked at each other and smiled. "The old medicine man was here in the cave with us and gave Jim a plate, indicating that we would be allowed to take it back with us to be translated," Julie said.

The Professor looked around. "Is he still here?"

"No, he's not; he's gone now," Jim said.

"We'd better be going now before we have to climb down this mountain in the dark and maybe get hurt in the process," Julie said, after a couple more minutes of looking around the cave.

"Let's get going, we need to make sure we leave no trace that we were ever here," Jim said.

As they left the cave, using a pine bough, they brushed their footprints away to make sure no one knew that they had been there as they made their way back to the trail. Making their way back down the trail was a little harder, simply because of the setting sun. Fortunately, the trail they were following down the mountain was easy to follow, with a full moon and a clear sky making it easier to follow. It took them about three hours of following the trail before they got to the base of the mountain, where the river could be seen and heard.

Arriving back at their camp, Julie started to prepare dinner for the three of them. Jim and the Professor were trying to decide what to do, as far as if they should go back to BYU now or wait and continue doing their work here at the dig. Julie, who was listening to the conversation between Jim and her dad, said, "I think what we have found is more important than whatever else we could find digging here in the dirt."

Jim and the Professor looked at Julie and thought about her words for a second. Both, looking at each other, agreed. "I guess that means we leave as soon as we can tomorrow or the next day back to BYU," the Professor said.

"The real question is, who do we show this plate to once we get back there?" Jim asked.

"And do we tell the world what we have found here?" Julie added.

Everybody looked at each other and as they thought about the question, Jim was the first to answer. "Let's not a make a decision on it until we learn what's on the plate that the medicine man gave us."

Julie and the Professor agreed with Jim on this. "I believe that's the right thing to do, not saying anything until more is known about what's on the plate. It may save some embarrassment for all involved, especially if there isn't anything of value on the plate other than a new language being found," Julie said.

Jim looked at the Professor. "When did she get so smart?"

"I think she gets it from her mother and maybe a little bit from me as well."

Julie smiled at both of them. "I most definitely get it from my mother and a little bit from my dad, seeing as how I live with him in the same house."

The Professor laughed. "Good recovery, Sis."

By the time dinner was over it was ten o'clock. With everybody tired from a long day of hiking up and down the mountain and emotions running high from finding the cave, everybody was ready for a good night's sleep, satisfied that what they were bringing back with them from the cave was better than anything they could have possibly imagined.

Chapter VI

The next morning started early with breakfast and loading the vehicles. After the two Jeeps were finally loaded, it was decided that Jim and Julie would drive one of the Jeeps and the Professor would drive the other. This way the Professor could listen to his opera music without Julie begging for him to stop the killing of the cats.

Jim liked having Julie ride with him simply because, being in love, it was hard to find some alone time for the two of them. Plus, they could listen to the kind of music they both liked, and that was country western, which the Professor thought was sacrilege. The Professor thought that if you played a country western song backwards, the guy would keep the girl, the dog wouldn't die, and the truck wouldn't break down. Otherwise, the music was about losing the girl, the dog dying, and his truck breaking down, and worst of all the bar being closed. Julie took it in stride, saying that her dad was right for the most part, but it was still what she liked to listen to.

The drive home to Utah was approximately a two-day drive. There were three different ways of driving from Colorado to Utah. One was cutting across a part of Colorado, then following Interstate 70 through to the town of Salina; another was to follow Interstate 70 to Interstate 15, then north to Provo. The easiest way was through Price and going through Spanish Fork Canyon. Any one of these ways was long and drawn out, simply because driving across eastern Utah was nothing but 110 miles of arid desert for the most part and then crossing over one mountain range in Utah. Staying the first night in Vernal, they found a room for the night and then they visited the Dinosaur National Monument in the afternoon. Dinosaur National Monument is a U.S. National Monument located on the southeast flank of the Uinta Mountains on the border between Colorado and Utah at the confluence of the Green and Yampa rivers. The park contains over 800 paleontological sites and has fossils of dinosaurs including Allosaurus, Deinonychus, Abydosaurus, from the Jurassic Period some 150 million years ago. The park is quite large and has barely started releasing her secrets of the prehistoric past to science.

The park was very interesting in that it was a collection of dinosaur bones that had been left behind in a mud pit that had fossilized. The bones in the pit looked like a giant jigsaw puzzle all mixed together with the paleontologists trying to put the right pieces together to create a complete dinosaur. Being an active site, in some cases, they send complete dinosaur skeletons throughout the world to other museums for display. Similar to the Dinosaur National Monument, the Cleveland-Lloyd Dinosaur Quarry, at the edge of the San Raphaël desert in south central Utah, is set up the same way but is handled by the Bureau of Land Management. The Cleveland-Lloyd Quarry is also well known for containing Jurassic-era dinosaur fossils, which include Stegosaurus, a possible ankylosaur, a prehistoric crocodile, two turtles, and four genera of snails. Both parks are known for their dinosaur bones all over the world; in fact, the velociraptor found at the Cleveland-Lloyd Quarry confirmed the size of the one used in Jurassic Park, the movie. As for the three of them, they would only be able to visit Dinosaur National Monument on their way back to Provo.

The next morning, they drove the rest of the way, driving through Price and then going through Spanish Fork Canyon to connect to the city of Spanish Fork and Interstate 15. From there it was a short drive to Provo. Once they saw the big white Y near Mount Timpanogos, they knew they were home. Getting in late in the afternoon, they all went to the Professor's place to get cleaned up and rest till the following day. In the meantime, the Professor started making phone calls to the Dean of the college over the department of archeology to set up a meeting with him for the next day. Until then they would rest and organize their findings.

The next morning, feeling better and rested, and most of all clean from the smoke of the campfire and being out in the country, they made their way to the BYU faculty building to meet with the Dean. After sitting down outside the Dean's office for a couple of minutes, all of them were excited to meet him, not because of him but what they had brought with them from Colorado. Jim, being the most excited, was holding the plate wrapped in cloth in his hands. The secretary went in to announce that the Wainwright party was outside waiting to see him. Coming back to her desk after closing the door behind her, she said it would be a couple of minutes and that the Dean would be with them once he finished his phone call. After a few minutes of waiting, the Dean opened the door and came out. He shook their hands and, grabbing the Professor, he invited all of them into his office. The Dean closed the door behind him, being the last to walk in. "So what was it that was so important that you cut your trip short to get you back here so quickly?"

"Well, I think you'll be happy that we did that after you see what we found not too far from where we were doing our dig," the Professor said.

The Professor looked at Jim and nodded, whereupon Jim unwrapped the plate and showed it to the Dean. "There were hundreds of these where we found this one. This was the only one we had permission to bring back," Jim said.

The Dean, taking the plate and looking at it and then looking at the Professor, saw him smiling and nodding his head. He picked up the phone and called Professor Jones. While the Dean was still looking at the plate, Professor Jones answered the call. "Can you come down to my office immediately," the Dean emphatically suggested.

Within minutes Professor Jones came into the Dean's office. "So why the rush to get me here?"

Handing the plate with the writing on it to Professor Jones, who stopped mid-sentence, looking it over himself, and then looking at the Professor and the Dean with a question in his eyes, to which they both nodded yes at the same time. Realizing what he was holding, a big broad smile appeared on his face. For the first time, everyone in the room realized what the they were looking at in Professor Jones' hands. Each of them knew and understood the ramifications of the discovery of the plate of gold and how it would impact all of the world of archeology with the possibility of changing the timelines of man in North America and possibly challenging what was thought to be known about man's existence on the earth.

Jim and Julie were surprised by the silence in the Dean's office, as each of the men held the plate in their hands. Looking at the writing on the plate, they started to use their education trying to decipher the writing symbols and each coming up with more questions than answers. By now all of them were sitting down around the Dean's desk. Once Professor Jones was over the shock of seeing the plate, all of them started talking at the same time, trying to ask their questions all at once.

Finally, Professor Wainwright raised his hand. "First of all, let me introduce you to the person who led us to the place where we found the plate. This is Jim Fowler; he is the one that found the cave where the medicine man's remains were found. Do you remember me sending the pictures of the cave and of the medallion he had found?"

Each of the two men realizing who he was, shook Jim's hand. "Welcome, and how did you find the cave?"

Jim went on to explain about finding the cave and the medallion and how Julie was helpful in taking pictures inside the cave, where they found the remains of the medicine man and the other artifacts. They then looked at Julie and shook her hand as well. As Jim continued on with his story, the two men couldn't take their eyes off the plate as they listened. Jim described in more detail about what they found inside the cave. The two men looked up at Jim at this point. "There's more plates and other stuff as well?"

The Professor nodded his head. "Hundreds more of them inside the cave plus Spanish gold and other gold artifacts."

The Dean looked at the other Professors, and he could see in their eyes what this would mean to the school, having found the mother lode of plates and the gold inside the cave. Thinking of the knowledge that would be found on the plates and knowing what it would mean to the world and BYU as a whole, the Dean asked, "There's more of these? Are you planning on bringing all of them back to the college?"

"I think we need to let the president of BYU know what we've got here," Professor Jones interjected before the Dean's question could be answered.

At this point Jim stipulated, "We are not allowed to bring any more back with us."

Both the Dean and Professor Jones looked surprised at what Jim had said and asked, "Why not?"

"Because now is not the time for this to come forth. We were lucky to be able to bring this plate back with us."

The Dean looked at Professor Wainwright for a minute, and then Professor Wainwright said, "I have to agree with Jim about this, we were lucky to bring this one back with us to show you."

"I don't understand this at all," Professor Jones said.

"It's like this: My job is to protect the cave from thieves and marauders who have ideas about getting the plates for their gold value and becoming rich. The records that are being kept in the cave are considered sacred, and it isn't time for the world to see them yet. When that will be, I really don't know at this time," Jim said.

"You see, it has become our responsibility to keep them safe from everybody that would want to use the records for their own purposes. You do remember how long it was before Joseph Smith received the gold plates to translate and how many times he had to hide them from the others that wanted them for the gold to get rich?" Julie asked.

"This is the same thing, except we are the ones being asked to keep them safe for the time being," Professor Wainwright added.

"I believe the time is coming very soon where these records will be brought forth and what is written on them will be shared with the world or at least with the church as a whole," Jim said, continuing, "I believe the world isn't ready for what is written on the plates just yet."

As each of them considered the importance of what Jim had said about protecting the plates they all had mixed feelings on the subject.

"Can you decipher what is written on this plate?" Professor Wainwright asked Professor Jones.

"I believe it can be done, although it may take some time to do so," Professor Jones replied, looking again at the plate.

"Think of it this way: once we figure out what is on this plate, maybe the time to translate the rest of them will come shortly thereafter. But until we get that permission, the plates are safe where they are for right now," Jim said.

"In the meantime, we do not need to announce to the world, leastwise just yet, that we have this plate. That way we have time to work on it without a bunch of reporters getting in our faces about it," Professor Wainwright said.

Picking up the phone, the Dean called the president of the university. "Do you have time to meet with me and some other people about something important?"

After a few more minutes on the phone and listening to the president, the Dean said, "Yes, we can be right over."

Hanging up the phone and looking at Professor Jones, the Dean said, "Please keep this under your hat for the time being; I'll let you know when you can have it to work on."

"I'll be waiting for you when you get back from the president's office," Professor Jones said, looking at all of them.

As the Dean took the three of them to the president's office, Professor Jones waited till they were out of sight before leaving for his own office. Closing his office door behind him, he quickly picked up his phone and speed-dialed a phone number. Once the person at the other end answered, Professor Jones spoke quickly and quietly. "Something has come up, I need to meet with you sometime tonight at our normal place." After the other person made a few statements Professor Jones said, "Fine, I'll meet you at seven o'clock tonight then."

Hanging up the phone, the Professor leaned back into his chair and smiled, thinking about how rich he would be, and famous too, for finding the lost cave full of gold, including gold plates on which the history of this part of world was written. He would be famous, and all the colleges would be begging him to come work for them. The colleges would be there for the choosing, to teach at or maybe become a Dean as well. Certainly, he would go down in history as the most famous and, not forgetting, the richest man in the world for finding the lost cave of gold. And best of all, nobody but the Professor, his daughter, her boyfriend, and himself knew about it.

The seeds of greed that were planted a long time ago, and had been dormant, were starting to grow again and rear their ugly head in the shape of Professor Jones.   You could bet he would keep this quiet, as he smiled to himself. That way he wouldn't have to share the gold with anyone else.

They didn't know it yet, but Jim, Julie, and her dad, were about to be tested in their loyalty to the medicine man and to each other and the promise each of them gave to protect the cave, no matter what.

At seven o'clock at the preassigned spot, Professor Jones met with his phone contact. Jones looked at the man, who was known to him only as Nesbitt, advising, "You need to watch over a couple of kids that just came back from Colorado. Don't do anything to them yet but watch them until I tell you otherwise."

Nesbitt nodded. "Who are they and where can I find them?"

"Find Professor Wainwright. He has a daughter named Julie and she is dating a young man by the name of Jim. These two know where the gold is, and I need you to watch them both, at least until I decipher the writing on the one plate they brought back with them," Professor Jones said.

"What then?"

"I'll let you know when I know more. There may be a chance to make some extra money if the two of them get in the way."

Nesbitt smiled when the Professor said that. "I'll be waiting for your word when it comes time," he said, as he got up from the table and walked out of the café.

Nesbitt was a sociopath that liked working in the dark; he found that it paid the best in his line of work of making people disappear for good. Professor Jones had used him before in other places and times, especially in his time as a young Professor starting out to get tenure at another university. The Dean had taken a disliking to him simply because the Dean recognized him for what he was as a bottom feeder looking to get rich and famous in the cutthroat business of archeology. Nesbitt was able to find incriminating evidence against his biggest opponent, the Dean, in getting a Professorship at the college he had started to work at back east. He was accepted for the Professorship only after the photos of the evidence showed up at the Dean's house, special delivery. From then on, the Professor had Nesbitt on retainer for cases like this one.

Moving to BYU was a calculated move to get in good with the department chair, to take his place. BYU was considered the foremost college in the nation when it came to the natural sciences department, to include archeology and paleontology. He even joined the Mormon church in order to get in good with the college. His move was for notoriety and acceptance in Utah and was calculated to springboard him to other major universities throughout the country. Using Nisbett's' special abilities, he tried to find dirt on the head of the department but couldn't find anything that he could use against him. Now he had to wait and find another avenue to travel in order to get where he wanted to go. Unbeknownst to him, Professor Wainwright had provided the answer to his dilemma. This gold plate he was about to decipher would work in his favor, even better than blackmail, and so much easier than digging for dirt like he had done on his previous employer.

Professor Jones figured he had covered all his bases by making sure that he would be part of the process of translating the gold plate, plus having the kids followed and maybe using them as leverage to find the cave. For the first time, he started thinking about all the fame and fortune that actually fell into his lap more by accident than on purpose. All he had to do was wait and see where the translation of the plate would take him. He laughed to himself, thinking how foolish Professor Wainwright and the two kids had been by telling the Dean and himself about the cave of gold, and how it would be their downfall. The best part was, all he had to do was translate the plate and he would become rich by getting rid of all three of them along the way.

Chapter VII

With the meeting completed with the president of the university they could tell that he was all excited about what Professor Wainwright and his two students had found in the cave. Agreeing with the Professor about keeping it quiet, leastwise until it could be translated, he also felt confident that between the Dean and Professor Jones they would be able to decipher what was on the plate. Professor Wainwright, with Jim's permission, left it in the hands of the archaeology department chair to allow them to start working on it immediately, for which Professor Jones claimed he would guard the gold plate with his life.

By now the photos, along with the notes that Professor Wainwright had sent back to the school when they were at the dig, were making the rounds through all of the other colleges and universities across the world. Professor Wainwright was curious if the theories that he had included would be accepted based upon the artifacts that his team had recovered from the dig. Most of the news that came back to him was more about the age of the artifacts as he showed the letters and emails from other Professors. "It turns out there is quite a bit of interest in what we've found, mainly from the other universities back east. Their biggest questions are, what made us decide to look into the cave on the face of a cliff, and how old are the remains of the bones we found in it?"

Jim and Julie let him shine for the moment, knowing that BYU would get credit for his and their work out in the field. It was fun watching the Professor get recognition for his life's work, finally. He was starting to get phone calls from other universities about being a guest lecturer at their own schools of archeology. The Professor's star was rising, and it was fun for Jim and Julie to see him smile about all of the notoriety he was getting.

Now that they were all back from the field, Jim and Julie had time to enjoy the downtime of not being on the dig. They were able to go out on dates and see movies and just enjoy each other's company. The Professor was lost in his own world, and that was fine for Jim and Julie, simply because they were lost in their own world as well. They were having fun being able to do things together. Going on picnics up

Provo Canyon and talking about their future together became the main topic for both of them. Being lost in each other's eyes, they didn't notice the man that had been given orders to follow the two of them. Right now, the world was just fine for the both of them. Some of the limelight fell on them as well, simply because the Professor was willing to share it with them for their part in discovering the cave and the plate. For the Professor, it wasn't about being in the limelight so much as it was about keeping the cave out of the limelight based upon the questions he was being asked about where they were found. For the two kids, it was enough to be part of something bigger and to protect the cave with their silence. Each of them knew they eventually would be going back to the cave to return the plate to its rightful owner. Until then, the world would have to be satisfied that the one plate would be enough to have. And who knows, there may be something of value on it after being deciphered.

The work of deciphering the symbols on the plate by Professor Jones progressed at a fast pace and eventually what was written on the plate started coming forth. Translating the symbols was easy after the first two lines were complete; from there it was a matter of finding the common symbols and then filling the gaps with the symbols not yet identified. It took about six weeks to do the complete plate, with Professor Jones working on it during the day when not teaching and also at night.

It seems that the plate told of a group of people who had lived in the area of the Royal Gorge and how they once roamed all of Utah, Colorado, and parts of New Mexico and Wyoming. They were part of a bigger group of people from the south that they had left behind, being prompted to move away from the main body to settle in an area that was completely different from what they had been living in. The people of the valley were basically nomadic, following their main source of food all year long in the lowlands, moving to the prairies during the winter months and then the high mountains in the late spring and summertime.

Their story starts off with a storyteller telling of the creation of the earth. The Great Spirit saw that there was nothing in space and, it being dark, decided to create a sun for light by snapping his fingers. Placing the sun on his right shoulder, he realized that he could see now, but there was nothing to see, and having the sun on his shoulder was really hot. The Creator then created rain and snow, and once he had done this, he placed it on his left shoulder. Now he was cool. Seeing that there was no earth, he took his magic staff and created a hole and he stirred in the hole for quite some time. After he was done the Creator wanted to see what he had created. Stepping into the hole, he looked around and saw snowcapped mountains and plains. As he stood there looking at the earth, he realized he was cold, so he took the sun and shining it through the hole, the sun started to melt the snow and ice and created rivers, streams, and the oceans.

Breaking a piece off of his magic staff, the Creator dropped it into the water and created fish to swim in the water. Seeing that it was good, he waved his staff across the whole earth and created plants and trees all over it. The Creator then waved his staff again and created birds to fly all over the earth. Breaking a piece off of his staff again, he placed it on the ground and created the animals. Seeing that his work was good, he rested once more. At that time, all of the animals got along well together; that is, until the coyote was created. Now the coyote was a trickster and he went about talking to some of the animals, saying, "Those animals over there are talking about you in a bad way."

"Don't be talking about us," said the first group of animals to the other animals after listening to the coyote.

Then the coyote would go over to the other group of animals and do the same thing to them, saying, "They're saying bad things about you."

By now, all of the animals were mad at each other and they started to fight one with another. When the Creator saw this, he was displeased. Knowing that the coyote was responsible for this, he created a bear, who would be king of the beasts. Asking the bear to rule over the other animals, he asked that the bear control the coyote when he got out of order. So, every night when the coyote would start acting up, the bear would come and sit on the coyote until he settled down.

The Creator's great plan was to create people and place them all over the earth. So, taking his magic bag, he gathered twigs from the different trees that were there. He took twigs from the black mamba, Russian olive, cottonwood, and Chinese elm trees. Putting them into his bag, he rested for a season. Now the coyote saw all of what the Creator was doing and was curious as to what was in the bag. Going over to check it out, he noticed it was moving and making noises. Not knowing what was in it, he cut the bag open with a knife. With that, the people inside the bag came running out of the bag. Seeing this, the coyote went about trying to put the people back inside the bag, but there were so many scattered about that he couldn't gather them all up. Not sure what to do, he ran away and hid himself from the Creator.

When the Creator came and saw the bag was open and had been cut, he was angry and, reaching into the bag, he found some people still in it. Being pleased that these people were still in the bag, he pulled them out and, holding them in his hand, he called them Ute people. He then blessed them to be strong and that they would be able to defeat all their enemies. He placed them in the mountains of the Wasatch Range, the Uintah Mountains, and the Rocky Mountains to be forever known as the mountain people.

Once this was done, the Creator called on the coyote, who, being obedient to his master, came out from his hiding place; and as he approached the Creator, he had his tail tucked between his legs. The Creator looked at the coyote, saying to him: "Because you have done this, you will have to howl at the moon as your penance forever." That is why at night you can hear the coyote howling at the moon, even today.

The last portion of the plate went on to explain that everything has a purpose in this life. Mother Earth plus water created all of the plants and animals, including human beings. At the moment of birth, when the child takes his first breath, he receives part of the spirit from the Creator, which makes the heart beat inside our bodies. With it comes a gift to be shared with others; that gift is the gift of self with a talent. The Creator went on to say not to covet other people's gifts but to learn what your gift is and use it to bless others. In the end all people die, and when that happens, the spirit leaves the body and goes back to the Creator to spend eternity with him.

One of the drawings on the plate was a representation of the medicine wheel, and on it were feathers on each side of the wheel that represented the animals of the earth. The medicine wheel made of red willow represented the circle of life with a cross in the center. One part of the cross, facing east, stood for the yellow man; the bottom part of the cross, facing south, stood for the red man; the left part of the cross, facing west, stood for the black man; and the top part of the cross, facing north, stood for the white man, the symbol signifying all nations are together.

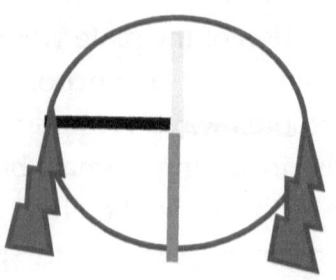

The people of the valley were deeply religious, and when they would have good hunting days they, of course, would give a prayer of thanks for their good fortune. They would pray before and after the planting and harvesting seasons, always giving thanks to the Great Spirit in the sky for everything they received from their hard work. The valley people were a peaceful people, who fought only to protect their way of life. The young men were skilled at war and were considered very powerful by the other peoples they met, and in all of their battles the Utes were never defeated. The valley people truly believed that the Great Spirit protected them from all their enemies. It was only when the white man, fleeing from religious persecution in the United States, settled in Utah with an agreement from President Lincoln, that the Ute Indians would be moved to the reservation, and they have been there ever since.

Chapter VIII

As Professor Jones was almost finished with the translation of the plate, he realized that it didn't say anything about the cave from which the plate came from. After all of his work in translating the plate, he was disappointed that the plate was just a story about the creation of the earth and the Ute people who lived in the Royal Gorge area, as well as Utah and New Mexico. Contacting the Dean and Professor Wainwright, after having completed the translation, they were each given hard copies of the translation and the symbols from the plate for their own use and to use as references. The university president received a copy, as well, showing the work that had been done. The leadership of the LDS church was excited to see the results, as well, after being told by the university president about the discovery of the plate. The leadership of the church was anxious to translate the other plates in the cave but were content to have this one plate to review. They knew the plates that were still in the cave would be coming forth soon enough and at the right time.

For Professor Jones, the right time was now, not in the Lord's time. Calling his man, Nesbitt he had him make up a plan of kidnapping the Professor's daughter. The time and place would still need to be worked out. Getting everything ready, finding a place they could use and a vehicle to accomplish the task, still needed to be done. That being said, this would be easy for Nesbitt to work out. Professor Jones wanted to make sure that he was being taken seriously when it came to finding the cave and the gold. Although murder wasn't on the agenda, it could easily be, if things didn't go the way he wanted them to. The question now on his mind was how to kidnap the girl and make good his threat without doing real harm to any of them, doing just enough to scare them and have them lead him to the cave.

Professor Jones would have Nesbitt kidnap Julie and have Jim roughed up to prove he meant business, nothing permanent, just a quick lesson in what he could do if they refused to play his game. Waiting for the right time and place for Jim and Julie to be alone, Nesbitt would be able to kidnap Julie without any problems and leave Jim as a message that he meant business.

This would entail Professor Wainwright being gone, leaving the two kids by themselves. As luck would have it, because of his work at the dig, Professor Wainwright received a call to come and be a guest lecturer at another university on the East Coast for one of their graduating classes. Receiving the invitation to speak, he cleared it with the Dean of the archeology department. The Dean approved his invitation to speak at the other university, and as a matter of courtesy, Professor Jones was notified. After hearing the news that Professor Wainwright was going to speak on the East Coast, he decided that now was the time for the kidnapping of his daughter to take place.

After seeing her dad off at the airport to go to his speaking engagement, Julie called Jim from her car. "Do you want to get together tonight and go do something?"

"I would like to go and see the latest *Star Wars* film, but I can't tonight. My schedule for tonight is busy because I'm doing some last-minute artifact logging from the cave of the medicine man that needs to be done for your dad," Jim said.

You could hear the disappointment in Julie's voice when Jim said he couldn't go. "How about tomorrow night we go see the movie, and you come over and help me with what I'm doing here?" he said, feeling bad as well.

"I'll be right over."

Parking her car in the school parking lot and realizing it was a long walk to her dad's office, Julie took a shortcut across the campus; and by doing so, Nesbitt missed getting her by about five minutes. Now driving to Professor Wainwright's house, the man waited all night for Julie and Jim to arrive. Instead of going home, Julie ended up staying at Jim's place while he slept on the couch.

Later the following evening, Jim was walking Julie back to her dad's house to drop her off at the door. They had just returned from seeing a movie on their date. As he stood there talking with Julie, she said to him, "Thank you for taking me to see the movie tonight; I really enjoyed it."

"It was my pleasure and thank you for helping last night on getting all those artifacts logged."

As Jim was leaning over to kiss Julie goodnight, Nesbitt, who had been hiding in the shadows, came up from behind Jim and hit him on the head, knocking him to the ground. Jim went down, hitting his head on the front porch step, and was out cold. Julie screamed and tried to run. Nesbitt, was prepared for this, blocked her escape and grabbed Julie, placing a cloth soaked in chloroform over her face, which she inhaled and then quickly passed out.

Picking Julie up and carrying her to the parked van, Nesbitt carefully placed her into the back of his van and closed the door. He came back and dropped the ransom note on Jim before going back to the van and jumping in the passenger side. Professor Jones, who was driving, quickly drove off with Julie in the back of the van. He was headed towards Interstate 15, looking for the Spanish Fork turnoff to find an old abandoned farmhouse. Nesbitt would stay at the farmhouse with Julie as his captive, to keep an eye on her and wait for the next step of the plan to begin. Having him keep Julie at the farmhouse wasn't a problem as she would be tied up and waiting as bait, waiting for Jim and the Professor to come through with the map of the location of the cave. The question now was, how long would they have to wait before taking another step to prove they were serious about wanting the information on the location.

The Medallion

When Jim came to after the van drove away, he had been out for about five minutes. He shook his head a little to clear the cobwebs from his brain. His head ached and, feeling around, he found two lumps on his head, one from Nesbitt and the other from the porch step. Fortunately, there was no bleeding from any of the bumps on his head. Picking himself up from the ground, the note fell down at his feet. Kneeling down to pick it up, he opened the note, which read, "The girl, for the location of the cave. Will contact you soon; don't call the police." Jim now started to worry about Julie being all right, not knowing where she was or who took her. He wondered what the captors would do if he refused to give them the location of the cave.

The first thing he did was look for Julie's phone in her bag that was left on the ground. He decided to call Julie's dad to let him know what had happened to her. Picking up the phone on the third ring, Professor Wainwright was expecting it to be Julie calling him, so he simply said, "You're late to be calling me tonight."

"This isn't Julie, Professor; it's Jim. I'm afraid I've got some bad news for you."

"What is it, what's wrong, what's happened?"

"Professor, Julie has been kidnapped and she's being held for ransom; that is, they'll release her if we tell them where the cave is."

Professor Wainwright, now sitting on the edge of the hotel bed, asked, "What happened?"

Jim went on to explain. "We were just getting back from watching a movie and I was dropping her off at your house. As I was talking to her on the front porch, someone came up from behind me and hit me on the back of my head, knocking me down. As I was going down, I hit my head on your front porch step and passed out. When I came to, Julie was gone and there was a ransom note left behind."

"What did the ransom note say?"

"It said, Julie's safe return for the location of the cave; don't call the police."

As the Professor was listening to Jim, he was wondering if there was any way to get home sooner than tomorrow morning. He had already had a flight scheduled out first thing the next morning to Salt Lake. In the end, the Professor resigned himself to the fact that the fastest way home was to wait overnight to catch the flight in the morning. For now, all the Professor could do was worry about Julie being okay.

"Should we contact the police?" Jim asked the Professor.

"I think we should sit tight, leastwise until we get the next ransom note to see how they want us to proceed from here."

Jim was beside himself with worry as to what to do with Julie being kidnapped, while waiting for the next note to come through. Jim also wondered who would do this. He knew that only five people, besides himself, would know about the plate and the cave. That was the Dean, Professor Jones, Professor Wainwright, the president of the university and, of course, Julie. Did any of the five who knew about the cave talk to someone they shouldn't have? Could the president have said something to someone else in passing? Three could be eliminated right off the bat because they were the ones who brought the plate with them. The other two, Professor Jones, who did the translating of the plate, and the university president, could be considered suspects. Jim thought about Professor Jones, knowing of the cave and what was inside it would make him rich and famous if he were to find the location. The university president wasn't above suspicion; however, that being said, it seemed ridiculous to Jim to risk the credibility of the university in order to become rich and famous. For Jim, the only person he considered who would do this would be

Professor Jones, simply because he was the newest Professor at the school and had the most to gain from finding the cave.

Jim's head was still hurting from being hit twice, and Julie being gone only made things worse for him. Deciding to head back to his place to take a couple of aspirins and lie down, all he could do was wait for the next ransom note to appear and be contacted by the kidnappers.

Jim picked up Professor Wainwright at Salt Lake City International Airport the following morning at ten o'clock. The Professor was traveling light with one piece of carry-on luggage, so there was no need to wait at the luggage return carousel. Passing by the luggage section, they went straight to Jim's Jeep. Jim updated the Professor. "No ransom note has been delivered as of yet from the kidnappers."

The Professor nodded, acknowledging what Jim had said. He could tell that Jim was just as concerned about Julie as well. Being just as concerned as Jim, and maybe more so because he was her father, his main thought was about Julie and how scared she must be finding herself kidnapped. The Professor was just as concerned as Jim was for her return. Neither of them spoke the entire trip back to Provo. The question on their minds was what to do about having to make a decision of trading the location of the cave for Julie's life. As they drove down Interstate 15, with no accidents to be reported on for once, traffic was normal for that time of the morning.

Chapter IX

Julie woke up from being drugged and she soon realized that she couldn't move her hands or feet. Looking down, she could tell she had been tied to the chair that she was sitting on. She soon realized that her mouth was covered with tape, making it impossible for her to scream out and let someone know where she was. Looking around the room, she didn't recognize her surroundings at all. Off in the distance she could hear cars and trucks going down what sounded like a highway. Knowing she was near civilization brought a little comfort to her. She also knew Jim and her father would be searching for her as well. Closer still, she could hear a radio playing a local station that she recognized from her dad's style of music. Trying to move her hands, feet, and legs, she found them taped down with duct tape, and it was wrapped so tightly around her that she couldn't move at all. At this point all she could do was wait for Jim and her father to find her, hopefully not dead.

Julie was feeling a mixture of emotions, she was scared, mad, and ready to cry, all at the same time. Being more mad than scared, she held back the tears as she focused instead on her surroundings, hoping to find anything that would help her escape from where she was. Looking about the room, she could tell that the room hadn't been lived in for quite a while. The walls were ripped, and in some places there were holes in the wall where she could see outside into the darkness of the night. The floors of the room weren't in any better condition, either; you could tell you had to be careful where you stepped so you wouldn't fall into the basement.

By now the door of the room opened and Nesbitt walked carefully into the room. Julie pretended to be asleep once more, closing her eyes waiting to see what would happen next. He was looking at Julie, trying to determine if she was still out from the chloroform he had given her earlier. Being impatient and not wanting to wait for her to wake up, he grabbed her by the hair, yelling, "Wake up, Julie!" ripping the tape from her mouth.

Julie screamed out because of the pain from how hard he had pulled her hair and having the tape ripped off her face at the same time. Now the tears began falling down Julie's face; all her pent up emotions finally came to the surface.

Looking at Nesbitt and seeing him laugh at her made her cry out, "Let me go!"

"I knew you were pretending to be asleep!" he said, sneering at her. Grabbing her by the hair again, he got real close and whispered in her ear, "Now that I've got your attention, I want you to understand the only thing keeping you alive right now is Jim telling us where the cave of gold is."

Julie opened her eyes a little wider and through the tears saw the man who was now standing over her. Now she was really scared from what he said. She could see a scar running down the side of his face from the bottom of his ear across his cheek. She closed her eyes, trying to forget his face.

Nesbitt laughed. "Ain't it a beautiful scar? This is nothing compared to what I have in store for you if your boyfriend doesn't come through with the location of the cave. In fact, I might still do the same thing to you, just for fun. It's been a long time since I've had that kind of fun," he said, as he pulled out his knife and put it against her cheek, carefully running the blade from her ear down to her neck.

By now Julie was crying out loud and could barely see Nesbitt through her tears. In between her sobs she pleaded with him, "Please let me go. I won't tell anyone anything about you, just please let me go."

"Did the big, bad man scare you?" Nesbitt said as he laughed, putting away his knife. "Well, you'd better be scared. If I were you, I'd be praying that your boyfriend and your dad do the right thing by you. Otherwise, it isn't going to be pretty for you. There won't be a happy ending for any of you, do you understand me, little girl?"

Julie closed her eyes, pretending none of this was happening, wishing that Nesbitt wasn't real and that this would all just go away. Hoping he would just disappear from her sight, instead Nesbitt grabbed her by the hair again and laughed. "I'm the real boogieman, and I will do what I said."

Nesbitt continued laughing at Julie as he put more duct tape across her mouth before leaving the room and closing the door behind him. For the first time in her life, Julie now understood what being scared and helpless really felt like. The worst of it all was she didn't know how long it would be before Jim and her dad would get there or if they would get there in time. All she could do now was hope and pray they would find her and take her out of this nightmare.

Chapter X

Getting back home to Provo, Jim pulled into the Professor's driveway and retrieved the Professor's carry-on bag. The Professor got out of the Jeep and started fumbling for his house keys. Jim, having pulled the bag out of the back seat, stood there waiting patiently. Once the Professor found his keys and unlocked the door, both Jim and the Professor walked into the house. Jim made a beeline towards the couch, while the Professor proceeded to check his telephone answering machine and went through the email on his personal computer. Finding no pertinent messages on his answering machine or email account and finding no ransom letters in the mail, the Professor came into the living room and sat down in one of the easy chairs facing the fireplace. Jim could tell that having Julie gone was hard on the Professor, having already lost his wife and not wanting to lose his daughter too. Jim could only imagine what must be going through his mind and, not knowing what to say or do, stared out the window.

Jim, sensing what the Professor might be going through, asked, "How many people knew about the gold plate we brought to the college?"

This question made the Professor stop dead in his thoughts, "Only the three of us, and the Dean, plus Professor Jones, were the only ones who had any idea about the cave and where we found the plate."

"I'm just wondering if any of them had anything to do with Julie getting kidnapped."

This made the Professor stop and think about each of the people he had known for the last several years. Carefully going through his mind for anything out of the ordinary about each of them, he couldn't come up with any ideas that would indicate any ulterior motives.

At this moment the phone rang, and the Professor rushed to pick it up, hoping it would be the kidnappers. "Hello, who is this?"

The voice on the other end of the phone identified himself as the Dean from the school. "Just calling to see if you got home safe and to see how the trip went."

"The trip went well, and I'm home safe and sound; in fact, we just walked in the door."

"That's good. When you get a chance, stop by and tell me about your trip; I'd love to hear about it."

"I'll do that, but it may take a couple of days to get back to you and give my report."

"No problem. I'll see you when I see you. Goodbye, Professor."

"Goodbye, Dean."

After hanging up the phone, the Professor sat back down in his chair and began again to try to figure out who might have kidnapped his daughter.

Looking at Jim, the Professor said, "Please tell me one more time what happened last night when you brought Julie home from your date."

"Well, Professor, it's just like I said. We were standing at the door talking about the movie, and the next thing I know I'm lying on the ground, coming around from being hit on the head. I found the note lying on the ground next to me; I picked it up and read what it said. Then I called you to let you know that Julie had been kidnapped."

"There is nothing else you can remember?"

"No, I don't remember anything else. I wish I did, but I don't remember anything more," Jim said, exasperated.

"I believe you may have something there, as to who else would know about the cave. The only others would be Professor Jones and the Dean. I personally don't think it's the Dean; I've known him for too long to think he would do something like this. So that just leaves Professor Jones to check out. The question is, how do we do that without alarming him?"

"I don't rightly know yet, but I'm working on it."

Professor Jones was sitting in a chair across from the Dean's desk when he had called Professor Wainwright at his house. The Dean looked at Professor Jones, "Wainwright just got home from his trip."

Professor Jones nodded his head and acted out that he was glad to have Wainwright back safe from his trip. In fact, it was he who had actually asked the Dean to call to see if Wainwright had arrived back home yet. Knowing that he was home, he continued to visit with the Dean for a couple more minutes before excusing himself by saying he had some papers to look at. Walking back to his office and closing the door behind him, making sure that no one could hear his phone call, Professor Jones contacted Nesbitt. "Initiate step two of the plan."

Nesbitt hung up the phone and went into the back bedroom to see if Julie was awake. Finding her asleep, he shook her to make sure she was awake. Julie, being tied up, had fallen asleep sitting in the chair, and when he shook her she screamed. The scream was muffled by the tape over her mouth so no one else could hear her. Now fully awake, Julie listened to Nesbitt as he whispered in her ear, "Now I'm taking the tape off of your mouth and I don't want you to scream. If you do, I will kill your boyfriend, then your dad. Do you understand? No matter what happens, they will die."

Julie shook her head in acknowledgment of what Nesbitt had said. She sat and waited as he took the tape off her mouth, hoping it wouldn't hurt as much as the last time. Ripping it off again, the tape left her skin raw and red around her mouth, which made it hurt even worse. She bit her lip in order to keep from screaming out in pain. Throwing the tape away, Nesbitt dialed the number to the Professor's house, and as it rang, he pulled out his gun and left it sitting on the table next to Julie. He looked at Julie. "Don't think I won't use it on you. Now do as you're told."

She nodded her head in agreement one more time and waited, hoping for her dad to pick up the phone. When he answered, Nesbitt put the phone to Julie's head. "Say something."

Not really knowing what to say, she started off with, "Daddy, this is Julie. Can you hear me?"

The Professor was starting to cry at the sound of her voice but maintained his presence of mind. "Are you all right? Have they hurt you?"

Jim, seeing the look on the Professor's face, ran to get on the extension phone. Picking it up quietly, he listened in on the conversation between the two of them.

Nesbitt pulled the phone away from Julie. "All right, you know she's alive, for how long depends on you and your cooperation."

"Yes, I know. What do you want from me?"

"My boss wants to know where the cave is where you found the plate."

"I don't know where the cave is; I have never seen it. The only one that has seen it is Julie's boyfriend, Jim."

Nesbitt grabbed Julie by her hair again and she screamed out loud so that the Professor could hear it through the phone. "Do you take me for a fool, Professor?"

"All right, all right, I get your message loud and clear. When can we meet to discuss the exchange for Julie?"

"We will be in touch with you. I just wanted you to know we have your daughter and you better know we mean what we say if you're thinking about holding back on the information or about calling the police."

"Yes, I understand. Can I talk to my daughter again?"

This time Nesbitt put the phone next to Julie's ear and mouth, and all she could say was, "Daddy, please help me; I'm scared."

"I love you, we'll find you," the Professor told Julie.

Nesbitt came back on. "Remember what I told you; we'll be in touch."

Nesbitt hung up the phone and, leaving Julie in the room, he forgot to cover her mouth as he walked out of the room, closing the door behind him.

Jim was listening on the other phone. He was trying to pick up anything that would indicate where they were holding Julie. Not hearing anything that would help, he set the phone back in its cradle. He himself was almost in tears from listening to Julie on the phone. Then Jim, realizing that Nesbitt was hurting Julie, started to get mad, realizing that there was nothing he could do at this point by staying at the Professor's house. He decided he needed to do something, even if it was wrong. Not knowing what to do, he knew he had to leave the Professor.

"Professor, I need to get out of here. Sitting and doing nothing is driving me nuts, especially with Julie being hurt."

The Professor knew that there was nothing he could say to stop Jim from leaving. "Be careful out there. Rest assured, we'll find her somehow."

Leaving the Professor's house, he got into his Jeep and drove back to the college campus. He sat and waited in the Jeep for Professor Jones to come out of his office building. Jim had been thinking that the Dean and Professor Jones were the only ones who knew about the cave and what was in it. The Dean, as far as Jim could tell, wasn't the type of man to be greedy, and after thinking about this for a minute, that left only one man that might do something like this, and that was Professor Jones.

After Jim had been sitting in his Jeep waiting for about thirty minutes he saw Professor Jones come out of the building. Walking to his car, the Professor got in and drove from the parking lot onto State Street, over to another street which had access to the interstate, stopping first to get some fast food at a local burger joint. Jim noticed Professor Jones was buying a lot of food, in fact, more food than one person could eat. Jim sat and waited while the Professor picked up his order of food. He continued following the Professor as he made his way to the interstate and then went southbound towards Spanish Fork. Taking the eastbound exit to the State Route 6 turn-off he past Kmart and headed towards Price through Spanish Fork Canyon. Jim followed Professor Jones as he went through the canyon towards Price. The Professor finally slowed down at the Thistle turnoff and turned right onto State Route 89 towards Fairview. Now driving through the old town of Thistle, or what was left of it since it had been flooded out, he stopped near an old abandoned house that once was part of the town of Thistle. The Professor drove his car off the state road and onto a dirt road, stopping near a solitary old house. He got out of the car and gathered up the food he had brought with him and went inside the old house.

Jim parked up on a hill near the turnoff to Route 89 and was watching from a distance. He waited and watched as the Professor walked into the house, being met by another man at the door. In fifteen minutes the Professor reappeared at the front door of the house and got back into his car, minus the sacks of food. He then headed back towards Route 6 into

Spanish Fork Canyon, turning right towards Provo.

Jim, who was out of his car, was lying in a field of tall grass to keep from being seen by the Professor as he drove by. He waited a couple of minutes for the Professor to go by before getting back into his Jeep and drive back to Professor Wainwright's house. When he got back to the Professor's house, he walked in and saw that the Professor was still sitting in his chair in the living room, and he could see that the Professor was still visibly upset about his daughter being held hostage.

When Jim walked into the house, he was smiling. The Professor looked at him. "Okay, what are you smiling about?"

"I think I found where they're keeping Julie."

The Professor jumped up from his chair. "What are we waiting for?"

"My thoughts exactly."

Locking the front door behind them, Jim and Professor Wainwright got back into Jim's Jeep and headed down the interstate to the Spanish Fork Canyon turnoff. As Jim drove he explained how he decided to follow Professor Jones from the university to an old house in what was left of the town of Thistle. Professor Wainwright was surprised by the fact that it was Jones who had planned all of this. It didn't make any sense that the Professor would be involved in something like this. Jim, seeing the look of bewilderment on the Professor's face said, "It's really interesting what money can do to people when they think they can get rich."

"Especially if they can steal or kill for it."

By now the sun was starting to go down and it was getting dark as they made their way to the house in Thistle. Jim reached under his seat, picking up his small 9mm pistol and gave it to Professor Wainwright to hold onto. Jim looked at the Professor as he handed the gun to him. "You may never know; we might need this."

The Professor, looking at the gun, thought to himself out loud, "I've never ever thought about shooting anyone till now."

"No one has ever kidnapped someone you love before, either."

The Professor nodded, agreeing with Jim.

"Knowing you will do anything to protect your loved ones from harm, when the time comes you never know what you'll be able to do until you're pushed to the breaking point," Jim continued.

Stopping at the entrance to Spanish Fork Canyon, near a gas station and a café called the Little Acorn, they waited for the sun to finish going down behind the mountains. As the sun headed into the western sky, the shadows of the mountains started edging towards the valley, and one by one the lights of the cars came on as they passed along the highway, eventually becoming all you could see in the night. Jim drove back onto the road, heading towards the canyon. Taking the Thistle turnoff, he found a place where they could park and not be seen. As they were getting out of the car, Jim saw a light turn on inside the house where he thought Julie was. Carefully Jim and the Professor, using the light from the house as a reference, made their way to the house as they walked down the side of the mountain. They stopped only after crossing some railroad tracks near the bottom, close to the house. They stood there for a moment, trying to catch their breath before moving in closer. Slowly, they made their way to the house to look inside. Jim went first, going from window to window, looking inside to see if he could find Julie. He found her inside the last bedroom in the back of the house. It was dark and all he could see was her form sitting in a chair in the center of the room. He could tell that she was tied up with tape. Jim, carefully opening the window, slowly made his way into the room while the Professor, holding the gun, watched for Nesbitt from outside the window. Putting his hand over Julie's mouth so as not to scare her, he made eye contact with her and whispered, "Julie, it's Jim and your dad. We're here to take you home."

Once she recognized who it was in the dark, by the voice, she nodded her head. Taking his knife out of his pocket, he cut the tape that held her in place and carried her to the window to let her out. Seeing her dad standing there outside the house, she ran to him and hugged him for what seemed like an eternity. Putting his hand to her lips, he motioned for her not to say a word. Jim crawled out of the window and then made his way to where the Professor was with Julie. Jim took Julie, who was having a little trouble standing, under one arm while her dad held her under the other arm and half-carried her to the Jeep. It was tough going back up the mountainside, but eventually they were able to get to where the Jeep was parked. Once everyone was inside and settled, they started driving back to the Professor's house. While all of this was going on Nesbitt, who was supposed to be guarding Julie, had fallen asleep and was oblivious to the fact that she was gone.

Julie, as she sat in the car, was now letting out all her emotions. She was crying and smiling at the same time, thanking her rescuers and not letting go of her father, as Jim drove them back to Provo. When she settled down a little, her father explained that it was Jim who had found her in the old house. Reaching over and kissing Jim, she kept saying thank you the whole time.

"I should rescue you more often just for your kisses," Jim said.

Julie smiled and laughed a little, feeling somewhat embarrassed by her actions in front of her father. "It's my way of saying thank you."

"I like it a lot."

Getting back to the house, the Professor had Julie go get cleaned up before asking her any questions about her ordeal. Once she came back downstairs from changing clothes and taking a shower, she felt more like a human being again. When she was sitting comfortably in one of the recliners in the front room, both Jim and her father started asking her questions, with Julie trying to remember everything about her ordeal and answering as best as she could.

Jim asked the first question. "Do you think you could identify the man who was holding you?"

"There is no way I can forget the man's face. He has a scar that runs from the bottom of his ear to his mouth."

"Did you see Professor Jones in the house?" her dad asked.

"No, I didn't see him at all. Is he involved in this?"

"Yes, as a matter of fact he is. He's how we found you, I followed him when he brought food to the house."

"I wouldn't be surprised if he orchestrated all of this," Jim replied.

"Evidently, Professor Jones was in all of this, trying to find the cave," the Professor added.

"What do we do now that we know who is behind all of this?" Julie asked.

"I don't know. Going to the police would be a waste of time at this point. He will deny everything and claim he is being set up by us," the Professor said.

"What should we do then to catch them at it? You know it won't take them long before they find out you're gone and try it again," Jim stated.

"The first thing we need to do is leave the house and stay away from it, leastwise till we come up with a plan to get this cleared up," the Professor said.

"How long do you think we'll need to be gone?" Jim asked.

"I figure probably at least a couple of days," replied the Professor.

Julie, looking at both of them, got up and headed towards the stairs to get her stuff packed for the trip.

"What are you doing?" Jim asked, looking puzzled.

"I'm going to pack for our trip."

Jim followed her up the stairs to keep her company while she got her things together. In the meantime, the Professor went to his room, found a suitcase, and packed some of his clothes into it.

After Julie and the Professor gathered their stuff together, they drove over to Jim's place to get some of his belongings together. Once this was done, they stopped at a convenience store to get some food and gas. Jim filled up the gas tank and was looking at a map. When Julie and her dad came out of the store with the groceries, Jim said, "Where to now?"

As the Professor looked at the map, thinking out loud he said, "Well, one thing for sure, we don't want to go back towards the cave. So we need to stay in the local area."

"Where can we go that's close by so that Professor Jones and his henchman won't be looking for us?" Julie asked.

"How about we go to a motel or hotel and stay there for a couple of days, at least until we figure out our next step?" Jim said.

"Where are we going to stay that they won't find us?" the Professor asked.

"How about in Salt Lake City, at one of their hotels downtown, where we can park the Jeep in one of those multi-parking lots near the mall?" Jim suggested.

"Do you think we can find one with a pool? Because I've packed my bathing suit as well." Julie asked.

"I brought mine too, figuring we would find one with a pool," the Professor said.

"You know Professor Jones won't stop until he has the location of the cave, and because of that we are at risk of being caught again by him or his man. I suggest that we stay in a hotel for a couple of days to figure out how to trap him and his buddy so that we can turn them in to the police," Jim said, looking at both of them.

"Let's get going before they find us again," the Professor said.

Getting back into the Jeep, they found the Interstate 15 turnoff from Fourth South and turned onto the highway, heading north to Salt Lake City to hide out.

Chapter XI

Nesbitt, waking up later in the night, walked into the back room to check on the girl and noticed she was gone and started freaking out. Checking where she had sat in the chair, he noticed that the duct tape holding her had been cut cleanly with a knife. He then started looking for her all over the house and outside in the yard. After looking for about fifteen minutes, it was clear that she was gone for good. Deciding to call Professor Jones to let him know what had happened, he knew that he would be in trouble for losing the girl. Professor Jones blew up upon hearing the news, yelling at Nesbitt, "How could this happen when you were right there to watch over her!?"

Holding the phone away from his ear, all Nesbitt could say was, "It's okay, we'll find her again, I promise."

Once he cooled down, the Professor started to think of another plan to find the cave. Just before hanging up the phone he told Nesbitt,

"Meet me at our regular meeting spot in a couple of hours and don't be late for your sake!"

"Yes sir," said Nesbitt, and as he closed his cell phone he thought to himself, *Maybe I need to get rid of the Professor myself.* A smile creased his face as he thought about this, saying to himself, *just be patient and when the time comes you'll know what to do.*

As Nesbitt got into his car, he drove from the house and went back to his apartment to get cleaned up for his meeting with the Professor. Once he was done, he looked at his watch, saying to himself, *Time to go meet the Professor.* Having worked with the Professor off and on for several years, he had come to loathe him for what he saw in him, an egotistical narcissist, and he had come to hate him because he reminded him of his abusive father. Then he thought out loud, "If it wasn't for the gold the Professor promised me, he would already be dead. Either way, this will be my last job for the Professor, dead or alive."

Jim, Julie, and her dad found a hotel room in the center of Salt Lake City to stay in while they were hiding out from the Professor and his man. After bringing their luggage in, they made themselves comfortable. Julie turned on the television to watch the local news and started eating some of the food they had brought with them. All of them settled down for the night on one of the two double beds in the room. Tomorrow would be the day to plan their next step. Tonight everybody would just sleep and catch up on what they had missed as they each dealt in their own way with the stress of the kidnapping. As the evening went on, for the first time, everybody was able to relax. Jim rested on the bed with Julie and watched the TV with her. Julie, feeling vulnerable, not wanting to be alone, snuggled close to him, not letting him go far from her. The Professor was already asleep lying on the other bed. Eventually the TV was turned off, and the only noise in the room was the air conditioner blowing out cold air as everybody fell fast asleep.

Nesbitt met Professor Jones at the regular meeting spot to discuss their next move. Not knowing where to look for the Professor or the kids now proved to be a problem for them. Professor Jones, as he sat in the booth opposite Nesbitt, was deep in thought about all that had happened and was wondering if his role in all of this had been discovered. Not knowing this, he was unsure as to how to proceed from this point on. Looking at his options, he felt that he had two choices: One was to get out of town and play it cool and wait to see what Professor Wainwright and the two kids would do, and the other was to assume that he was still in the clear and act as if nothing had happened.

In reality, the only option that Professor Jones had was to assume that he was still in the clear, so he would continue acting as if nothing had happened. There was no other choice that could be made at this point. Only time would bear it out on his decision. Nesbitt, looking at the Professor, now saw him for what he was, a loser who would do anything for himself and damn anybody that got in his way. He had worked for other people like the Professor before but with money always up front, not promises of getting rich. He had taken a chance with the Professor because he was believable, and the thought of having all that money was too hard to pass up. The Professor was getting on his nerves, more so since Nesbitt had lost the girl, and he knew he would need to terminate him soon, but not just yet. The Professor might still fill a purpose for Nesbitt, especially if he actually did find the gold in the cave. Keeping the Professor alive long enough for him to find the gold seemed a better option. Once the gold was found, he could take care of the Professor and not have to split the gold with him.

After their meeting it became apparent that the best thing they could do was wait for the Professor and the two kids to surface again. Until then the Professor would go back to work at the college and act as if nothing had ever happened, hoping nobody would be the wiser for it. Hopefully, Wainwright would call the Dean to check in with him and explain why he wasn't coming in, thereby tipping his hand as to where he was. This way he would be there to find the three of them once again. This time he would do it right, without Nesbitt screwing it up for him.

The next day Jim and Julie were the first to wake up. They went quickly down to the restaurant to get some breakfast while the Professor continued sleeping. They left a note as to where they were going so that if the Professor woke up and they were still gone he wouldn't worry about them. As they sat there eating their breakfast, the Professor came down to the restaurant to get something to eat as well. Finding their table, the Professor joined them.

"Did we wake you?" Julie asked.

"No, not at all. The maid came in after she knocked on the door to come clean the room. Seeing your note, I came down to get some breakfast as well."

When the waitress finished taking his order, he sat there drinking his ice water and was deep in thought. You could tell he had several thoughts running through his mind. "It seems it might have been better to have stayed on the dig instead of coming back home, don't you think?" he said a minute later, smiling.

"No, not really. Look at all the fun we've had since we've been back home. I got kidnapped, two knights in shining armor rescued me from the bad guys, and look at us now, living the good life in a fancy hotel. What more could a girl like me want or ask for?"

The two men at the table looked at each other and laughed together about Julie's statement. Both looked at each other, trying to decide how to answer her.

"I believe this is where I say, are we having fun yet?" Jim said.

"And I say, you ain't seen nothing yet. Just because our fun meters are pegged doesn't mean it's over yet," the Professor added.

As they continued eating their breakfast, they started thinking about the next steps they would need to take to catch Professor Jones in a trap. This wasn't going to be easy, but in order to survive they had to plan accordingly. All during breakfast they talked about different scenarios they could come up with. The first one was to come out of hiding and let Jones and his man find the three of them and then be caught again to be held for ransom to find the cave. The next scenario was to tell the police about the kidnapping and turn them in for the crime. The final scenario was to lead them to the area of the cave and kill both men in the process. All had good points, and then again they all had bad points as well.

When they were finished discussing the scenarios, they went back to their hotel room and decided to go swimming in the pool. As the Professor sat by the pool on one of the loungers, he started thinking about the options in each of the scenarios and began formulating a plan. As he watched Jim and Julie having fun in the pool, playing and swimming with each other, he came up with an idea that would catch the Professor and his man. He knew that the motivating factor for Professor Jones was his greed, and that would be his downfall. Everybody must be willing to go the distance on the plan to make it work.

As Professor Wainwright continued watching Jim and Julie playing in the pool, he sat there, then for the first time he realized how much Jim loved his daughter and how much he wanted to protect her from the world of people like the Jones. At this point the Professor realized that he was tired of working for nothing in a world that only cared about being rich and famous. Motioning them over to where he was at the pool, he said, "You guys keep having fun. I need to run a few errands this morning and I'll meet you both back at the room when I'm done."

Jim, looking at the Professor, asked, "Is there anything I can do to help you?"

"Oh no, I can handle this myself. You stay here and enjoy yourselves in the pool."

By now Julie came up and splashed water on Jim and swam away from him just as quick. This got Jim's attention and he swam after her, trying to catch and splash her as well. The Professor walked out of the pool area and went back to the room to start running his errands.

An hour later Jim and Julie headed back to the room, and as they walked in Julie froze as she recognized the man sitting in the chair watching the television while Professor Jones was talking to her father. Professor Wainwright introduced both of the two men, "I want you two to meet my new business partners in what I hope will be a very good business deal for all of us."

Jim and Julie were both stunned by what her father had said to them. Seeing their surprise, the Professors laughed at the same time. "How do you think we found you the night I had you kidnapped?" Jones asked.

"You did that to me for the gold in the cave?" Julie asked, looking at her dad in shock.

"Oh, come now, did you really think I would let you get hurt? Do you realize how hard it is to make a name for yourself in the world of archeology? Why don't you tell her, Jim?"

This time Jim went from Julie's side and walked over to where Wainwright and Jones were standing. Looking at Julie, he started laughing with Wainwright and Jones. Julie, feeling hurt and mad, walked over to Jim and slapped him across the face. Jim wasn't surprised by her reaction, "Oh come now, is that how you treat the one you love?"

Julie, looking at him, shuddered in total rejection, "I could never love a man like you, you filthy pig."

Jim mocked being hurt and started laughing again at her for being so naive. Jim looked at Jones and Wainwright. "I think we're not getting married anymore."

Nesbitt stood up, "So when do we go get the gold from the cave and split it up?"

"Patience, my dear man, patience. We'll get the gold in due time," Jones said.

"Why don't you show my daughter to the bathroom, so she can change her clothes. Then we can get on the road to go get the gold and start living the good life," Wainwright said, looking at Jim.

Jim walked over to where Julie was standing and started to escort her to the bathroom to change her clothes. As he reached for her, Julie cringed and walked away from him. Seeing her reaction to Jim, they all laughed at her. "I think I should be hurt by her actions; what do you think, Professor Wainwright?" Jim asked.

"And here I thought I was gaining a son-in-law. What must I have been thinking? Well, you know what they say, 'All's fair in love and war,'" the Professor said. "Now, Jim, escort her to the bathroom, will you please. Julie, do hurry, we need to be on the road soon."

"I can't believe she thought I was doing this all on my own," said Professor Jones, looking at Julie.

"Well you know how trusting kids can be when they love their parents."

"Or their boyfriends."

Jim stood outside the bathroom door while Julie changed into her regular clothes. Jim was the next to change. While he changed into his clothes the Professor had Julie pack her bags, along with Jim's bag.

While Julie had been in the bathroom changing her clothes, she was speechless about finding out that her father and boyfriend, Jim, had been in on this the whole time. What bothered her was the fact that she couldn't tell when they were talking to her about doing the right thing in protecting the cave from Professor Jones and Nesbitt.

She thought to herself, *something must have happened while I was being held hostage at the house.*

But what it was she didn't know; all she knew was what she saw right now, right here. Coming out of the bathroom, Jim went in next and changed clothes for the trip. Taking only a couple of minutes to do this, they were ready to go within the hour. Using two vehicles, both Professors rode in the truck and Jim and Julie rode in the Jeep with Nesbitt in the back seat. Driving south towards Spanish Fork, looking for the Price turnoff, they made their way towards Price, looking for Interstate 70 once again. Continuing to the city of Price and stopping to get gas and some food, Jim asked Nesbitt to keep an eye on Julie while he went in to pay for the gas and pick up some groceries. Nesbitt smiled at Julie. "Maybe I'll keep you for myself when all of this is done. Why should Jim have all the fun?"

Julie started to get mad. "I'd rather die first, before you touch me in any way."

"Be careful what you wish for, you might just get it little lady," Nesbitt said, upset by her comment.

By now Jim and Professor Jones were walking back to their vehicles and could see that Professor Wainwright was just putting the gas-pump handle back in its cradle. Professor Jones had also picked up some drinks for him and Professor Wainwright to have for the rest of the trip, and he climbed back into the truck. He waved at Jim to let him know they were ready to start again. Jim acknowledged him by waving back. They drove back onto the highway, going through Price on the expressway that bypassed the city and headed towards the Interstate 70 connection near Green River. They then went on to Grand Junction, Colorado, and from there to Montrose and Salida, then to Royal Gorge. Driving all night, they made it to Royal Gorge early the next morning before daylight. Stopping where the base camp had been for the original dig, they set up camp once more. Leaving the vehicles behind, they took only what they needed on their backs.

Chapter XII

The team was ready in a few minutes after getting their gear from the back of the vehicles. As they were getting ready to go, both Jim and Professor Wainwright said, "We want you to know we have only been to the cave once and can't promise that we will be able to find the cave right off."

"We'll take our chances and follow your lead," Professor Jones said.

As he started loading his pack onto his back, Jim took the lead to find the trail that led to the cave, following the path next to the river. Jones was behind him with Wainwright next in line and Julie following her father, with Nesbitt bringing up the rear.

It wasn't long before Jim stopped, and pointing out another trail to Professor Jones, said, "This is the trail I told you about that threw me off the first time we were looking for the cave."

"Where does it go?" Professor Jones asked.

"Nowhere, I suppose; leastwise that's what we figured after following it for a mile or so. It turned out to be a deer trail. The trail we're looking for is further up this way."

With Jim still in the lead, they continued following the river, looking for the right trail. Jim was careful to point out more than one trail to Professor Jones as they made their way. This way Jones would be confused and not remember which was the right trail. At this time Julie started to notice that the trail they were looking for was behind them; in other words, Jim was leading Professor Jones on a wild goose chase. Looking at her dad for a second, she saw that he winked at her. Not sure as to what to make of this, she kept quiet about her thoughts and actions, being uncertain and confused by all of this.

Jim took the group another mile up the road before turning off the river trail. They now started moving inland and climbing, following the trail up into the mountains. The trail was beginning to get hard to follow. It was nothing more than a deer trail, and that was what Jim was hoping for. By all looks of it, this deer trail would lead nowhere, which is what Jim was counting on. Wainwright was playing along with Jim on this. "You see that over there?"

(pointing towards a mountain) "That's what I saw in my dream from the old medicine man when he was pointing out the way to find the cave."

Now, as Julie was listening to her father, she knew things weren't what she had thought they were, simply because she and Jim were the only ones who had had the dreams. Deciding to play along, she said nothing at all. The climb up the mountain was taking its toll on everybody, especially on Nesbitt. Although he wasn't saying anything, he was falling further behind more and more now, and as the rest of them would wait for him, he would need longer to recover. This was fine for Jim and Wainwright, simply because they both knew he was the one carrying a gun with him and having him tired made it, so he couldn't shoot straight if the situation ever arose. Professor Jones was holding his own, simply because the gold is what kept him going on. The thought of getting rich made him more eager to climb and hike the mountain trail.

By now it was three o'clock in the afternoon and everybody was tired. They had reached the summit and were now taking a break to eat what they had brought with them. Jim kept moving while everyone ate their food. He pretended he was looking for the cave or at least a trail to follow. Coming back after being gone for a while, he told the Professors that the trail was up ahead, and it wouldn't be long now. Waiting for everybody to finish eating their food and making sure everyone was ready to continue, they started on the trail again.

Unbeknownst to everybody, Jim had made contact with some of the local Indians, who had been up on the mountain fishing and camping. Recognizing the medallion Jim was wearing, they knelt down in front of him. Jim raised the leader of the group from off his knees, asking who he was. "My name is Red Hawk, and these are my brothers, Running Bear, Grey Cloud, and Big Eagle," the leader replied.

"I need you guys to do me a favor," Jim explained.

"What can we do to help?" one of the Indians asked.

"Well, what I want you to do is scare the hell out of these two guys that want to steal the sacred material in the cave."

All of the men looked at Jim and smiled. "Can we take some scalps?" the leader asked.

"No, in fact, I don't want any of them hurt, just scared really good."

The leader said, as he looked at the others who were still smiling, "We get to mess with the white man for fun? I want you to know you just made our day."

"I'm glad I did. Now the ones I don't want you to scare is the woman and her dad. You can tell the dad from the others because he is the oldest one of the three of them. Now be careful of the man in the back. He has a gun and he isn't afraid to use it, okay?" Jim said, smiling at them.

The group of Indians started looking around for some things that they could use to scare the two men. After about ten minutes of searching they found what they were looking for. The Indians were now ready to start having some fun. "We'll probably be staying here overnight, so you may want to make use of the dark," Jim said.

"It's going to be a long night for you guys," Big Eagle said, laughing.

The Indians, being led by Red Hawk, started off in the direction of the group of fortune hunters. When Jim got back to the group, he winked at Wainwright, "Are you ready to go yet?"

Jim helped Wainwright up from where he was seated and said in a very low voice, "I found some friends out there and they're willing to help us out. You might want to pass it on to Julie, so she doesn't get too scared; that is, if and when you can."

Wainwright stood up and nodded his head in agreement and started making his way up the trail. Pretending to slip on some rocks, he acted like he twisted his ankle and sat back down, calling out for Julie to come help him. Julie did as she was told and, walking over to him, leaned down and looked at his ankle. Jim kept the other two men moving up the trail.

"You guys go ahead. We'll catch up with you in a minute," Wainwright said.

As Julie looked at his ankle, Wainwright said, "Just so you know, Jim has met some friends up here and they're about to start scaring everybody."

Julie nodded her head and said out loud, "I can't believe you hurt your ankle, you stupid old man. If it was up to me, I'd leave you here to feed the coyotes!"

"Now, is that any way to talk to your father?"

"It's the way it is; you betrayed me. All you care about is the gold and not about me, and now you want me to help you steal the gold in the cave!"

Professor Jones, who could hear her scream at Wainwright, just laughed. "I wonder how much counseling it's going to take for her to get over what her dad did to her."

"Probably all of his share of the gold," Jim said.

"I believe you're right on that one."

Julie and her dad finally caught up with the others as Jim was explaining, "Now, where we are at is considered to be sacred ground and you might hear and see things that may surprise you."

Jones and Nesbitt looked at each other and laughed out loud, like this was going to really scare them away from the gold. Nesbitt pulled his gun out and said as he looked around, "Bring it on. I'm ready for them."

Red Hawk motioned for Grey Cloud to move in close enough to start throwing rocks behind them and then in front of them. Professor Jones almost got hit by one of the rocks that landed near him. Now Jones was wide awake and looking all around the place, trying to see where the rocks were coming from. He was now wondering if what Jim had said was true. He was getting nervous about the rocks that were being thrown at him. Nesbitt was watching Professor Jones and smiling as he watched him dodging the rocks while trying to stay on the mountain trail. While he was watching Jones he got hit in the arm by a rock himself. Now it wasn't so funny anymore. He then began looking around also.

Jim kept looking around the area as he traveled, searching for anything that looked like a cave. Moving further up the trail while Jones was dodging the rocks, Jim made contact with Red Hawk and signaled him that they needed to talk. As Jim kept moving up the trail, he could see Red Hawk in one of the bushes next to the trail.

Bending over to retie his shoes, Jim asked, "Is there a cave around here that would be big enough to hide a treasure in it? We need to find a cave that will work for me to lead these guys to."

"It just so happens there is a cave behind the waterfall that will fit your needs. It's deep but empty. We used to camp there a few summers ago. You'll see it as you follow the river aways up the trail," Red Hawk replied.

"Thanks for the information."

"You're welcome. How are the two guys handling being stoned naturally?" Red Hawk said, laughing as he made his way back up the hill, not waiting for a reply.

"Real cute, real, real cute."

Jim, now standing up and looking at the group, said, "It's just a little farther down by the river, near the waterfall."

Both Julie and her father were relieved that there was a cave close by. Looking at each other, each of them breathed a sigh of relief at Jim's words.

By now it was five o'clock in the evening and the sun was starting to go down, and everybody could feel the temperature start to drop with the setting sun. Jim was the first to find the river. Taking Julie with him, they searched on one side of the river while the Professors searched on the other side. As they started to go their separate ways, Nesbitt sat down on a rock. "When you find the waterfall, come get me. I should be rested by then."

As Nesbitt sat on the rock resting and trying to catch his breath, he heard a noise coming from one of the trees next to him. Turning just in time to see a rock coming at him, he jumped out of the way and slipped on the rocks, losing his footing and falling to the ground. Big Eagle and Running Bear quickly grabbed him. Keeping him pinned to the ground, one of the two braves then grabbed his gun. Big Eagle and Running Bear were wearing the traditional Indian dress for warriors from the past. Each had buckskin leggings on and were wearing black war paint, which covered their forehead and eyes. Nesbitt could tell that they were Indians as they put a sack cloth over his head. They carried him up to a stand of trees and tied him to one of them. Having him bound and gagged, they took his shoes and left. He could only sit there and wait, hoping someone would realize that he was missing and come look for him and untie him from the tree. He prayed that it wouldn't be too long of a wait.

Jim and Julie found the waterfall first and started searching the area for a dry entrance to the cave. Wainwright and Jones were still further back on the trail, so they couldn't see the waterfall yet. Looking around, Jim figured the entrance to the cave must be through the waterfall itself. Taking Julie by the hand, they walked through the falls and into the cave. As they entered the cave, both of them saw that it was big and empty. With no one being able to see behind the waterfall, Jim grabbed Julie and kissed her. This surprised Julie, who catching herself, kissed him back.

Jim looked at her. "I'm sorry for having to play you for a fool. Jones was spotted by your dad while we were swimming at the pool the other day. That's why he had to leave and run some errands."

"How did they know we were there?"

"Your dad called the Dean, letting him know where we were."

"Why would he do that?"

"So that we could set Jones up and do what we're doing now, leading them astray. We figured it was better for us this way because we control what's happening instead of them. Being here, the cave is safe and we're leading them on a wild goose chase."

Julie looked up and touched his cheek. "I'm sorry for slapping you like I did. You made me mad. Does it still hurt?"

"I deserved it for saying what I said to you. I had to make it look good for our audience. Evidently, they bought it all the way."

"Well, if it's any consolation, I hurt my hand on your hard head, so I guess that makes us even for the pain. One other thing: Don't ever do that to me again. I'll hit you twice as hard next time."

"And hurt your hand worse? I don't know if it's worth it. You already know how hard my head is."

They both laughed at Jim's remark and, kissing again, they started looking through the cave. With flashlights on, they walked deeper into it. The cave itself was quite large, in fact, the whole team could sleep in there and be comfortable. Finding nothing but fish bones and some rusty tin cans, they then looked at each other. "Well, what do we do now?" Jim asked.

As Jim and Julie went back through the waterfall, they came out just in time to see both Professors standing on the other side of the river bank near the waterfall. "Well, is it in there?" Jones asked.

"No, it's all gone. All we found was just some old fish bones and tin cans that were left in there. They must have moved the gold while we were in Utah."

Professor Jones, not wanting to believe his ears, went through the waterfall and started searching the cave himself. He came out about five minutes later, surprised that it was empty. Jones, looking at Wainwright and the other two, was furious, thinking that he'd been fooled by Professor Wainwright with the help of Jim and Julie, his daughter. He yelled at them, "You guys lied to me and now you're trying to cheat me out of the gold!"

"We are just as surprised as you are that the gold isn't there," Wainwright said.

This did not appease Jones. "You're just trying to hog all of the gold for yourself!"

At this point, Jim interrupted the two of them. "Look, the gold was here. Evidently, somebody else knows about it as well, and they must have taken it for themselves."

Jones was trying to locate Nesbitt, so he could have him take care of the three of them permanently. Calling out for him, he stopped mid-sentence, asking, "Where is Nesbitt?"

All of them, looking around, saw that Nesbitt was not to be found anywhere near the waterfall. Now a search was started to find him. They started backtracking down the trail to where they last saw him. Staying close to the river, once more they came to where they had left him sitting on the rock resting. Realizing he wasn't there anymore, they started searching the surrounding area near the rock. Jim and Julie were calling out to him as they moved about looking for him. Professor Wainwright, as he was looking for him, heard him first, and telling everybody to stop yelling, the Professor called out again. This time, Jim heard a noise coming from a stand of trees a little way up the mountain. Pointing in the direction of the noise, he started climbing up the mountain. After searching around Jim saw that Nesbitt was tied to a tree. Calling to everyone else, they all began to make their way up the mountain. Jim, reaching Nesbitt first, used his knife to cut the ropes that he had been tied to the tree with. Nesbitt stood up with the assistance of Professor Jones, as Julie and her dad took the blindfold off and the gag out of his mouth, while Jim cut the rope from around his feet.

Nesbitt was shaken up by what had happened and was still trying to stand up when Jim asked him, "What happened, how did you get tied up to a tree?"

"Two Indians dressed in war paint and buckskins grabbed me before I could react. The next thing I knew is that they had my gun and they were dragging me up this hill to tie me to this tree. Then they took my shoes and left me here blindfolded and gagged."

Professor Jones, looking at Nesbitt, laughed. "Two Indians dressed in war paint and wearing buckskins? You sure you weren't using some kind of drugs or smoking something?"

Nesbitt nodded at Professor Jones. "They even spoke in their own Indian language."

Julie came up to where the men were gathered, bringing some shoes that she had found sitting near the rock. "Are these your shoes?"

Nesbitt looked at them. "Yes. Where did you find them?"

"Sitting right next to the rock you were sitting on."

Now everybody was looking at Nesbitt as if he was hallucinating or was losing his mind up here in the mountains. Jones, waiting for Nesbitt to put his shoes on, said, "Now you're going to tell me they got your gun too?" Nesbitt looked at Jones and reached into his coat pocket, pulling out his hand with nothing in it and nodding his head in the affirmative with a look of what do you want me to say on his face. Jones was furious. "I can't believe they got your gun too." He walked off, leaving Nesbitt behind while muttering under his breath. Nesbitt quickly caught up with Jones and the two of them followed the rest of the team back to the waterfall, with Jim taking the lead.

Nesbitt was feeling frustrated by what had happened to him. All he could say was that he was sorry. Jim and the other two were now aware that the playing field was now level, being that the gun was gone. Professor Jones had no real advantage anymore when it came to the game being played now.

Jones started to cuss at his rotten luck, saying to himself, *"No gold, no gun, what else could go wrong?"*

Jim, hearing Professor Jones talking to himself said, "We're going to be sleeping here for the night; it's too late to head back to camp. I don't want any of us to risk breaking a leg or falling down the mountain walking back in the dark."

"Oh great, now were going to spend the night up here. Can we at least build a fire for the night to stay warm as I'm still soaking wet from the waterfall?" Jones asked.

Jim looked at Professor Jones. "Yes. All we need is some firewood, so we can build a fire. Let's spread out and see if we can find some wood."

Everybody now started looking for wood, going off in different directions to do so. Within minutes there was plenty of wood to last the night. Jim began building the fire with kindling, then added some bigger pieces of wood to it. The fire took off, and within minutes Jim was adding the bigger pieces of wood to keep it going. For Jim and Julie, the fire felt good as they stood there next to it in their wet clothes. In fact, Jones quit complaining, now that he was warming up next to the fire as well.

As they continued to look for more wood, Professor Wainwright walked with Julie. Once they were far enough away, Wainwright took Julie by the arm. "I'm sorry about being rude to you the other day. I had no other choice but to do it and play along."

Julie interrupted her father. "Jim has already explained to me what happened. I'm sorry for all the things I said to you over the last couple of days. I should have known better than not to trust you."

"I'm sorry to have you in the middle of all this. I wish there could have been another way without you having to be involved."

"It's okay. I can't think of a better place to be than being here with the two favorite men in my life."

The Professor smiled and let her go as they continued looking for more wood for the fire. As the fire was built up, the night was falling fast and the chill in the night was pretty evident to all of them. They all gathered around the fire to stay warm. Jim had everybody take off their backpacks and bring whatever food there was and put it in the center of the ground. Finding nothing to cook, Jim decided to try his luck at fishing, taking his shoelace from his boot asked, "Do any of you have a safety pin I could use?"

Professor Wainwright produced one from his backpack, "These are nice to have around to use in a sling in case you hurt your arm."

Jim, taking the safety pin, opened it up and attached it to the shoestring. He then went down to the river and started lifting rocks near the water, hoping to find some bait to use. Finding some earthworms, he hooked one of them on his safety pin and sat down next to a deep pool in the river and put the pin and worm into the water, letting it sink. Waiting a few minutes, he had a strike. He pulled the fish out of the water and laid it on the bank next to him. Attaching another worm to the safety pin, he put it back into the water and waited for another strike. Within a short period of time he had caught four fish from the deep pool. Coming back to camp, he gave the fish to the Professors to clean and cook for dinner. Jim went back out to see if he could catch some more fish for himself now. He thought to himself, *leastwise we won't starve tonight*.

Coming back into camp with two more fish, Jim could see the fish were being cooked on some sticks over the fire, and adding his two fish as well, everybody was able to eat that night while saving the food from their backpacks for tomorrow.

Jim, Julie, and Professor Jones were seated closest to the fire, still damp from their waterfall experience. All three of them were sitting pretty close to each other to try to stay warm. For Jim and Julie, this was normal for the type of summer they had already experienced while at the dig site.

By nine o'clock everybody was tired and ready to sleep. It had been a long two days of no sleep and hiking up the mountain. All was quiet in the camp. The fire was burning bright and each of the team found a comfortable place to sleep for the night. Jim cut some pine boughs down from the trees and laying them out on the ground made a place that was more comfortable to sleep. Julie gladly accepted the pine bed and lay down next to Jim, who was removing some rocks from under the boughs before he lay down, finally certain that all the rocks were gone.

Within minutes everyone was sound asleep, dead to the world. Just before falling asleep, Jim leaned over and kissed Julie good night, who was already half asleep. She smiled at Jim and mumbled, "I love you."

Jim looked up into the night sky, saw the Big Dipper and the North Star, and wondered to himself how all of this was going to turn out in the end.   As he lay there watching the sky, a falling star crossed over the campsite into the horizon.   With that, he fell sound asleep.

Unbeknownst to the sleepers, Red Hawk and his brothers were waiting in the shadows.

Chapter XIII

Red Hawk and Grey Cloud had been waiting for everyone to settle down and go to sleep. Quietly sneaking into camp, Red Hawk and Grey Cloud, each carrying a water snake in a bag, carefully pulled the snakes out and placed one of the snakes on Professor Jones' leg. The snake slithered past his lap and coiled itself up on his warm belly, ready to sleep for the night. The other snake they placed on Nisbett's' shoulder, and it went down into his shirt to find a warm spot. Quickly the two Indians left the camp, disappearing into the darkness.

As Nesbitt lay there, something started tickling him. Being so tired, it took a couple of minutes for him to realize something was making him laugh. As he woke up to being tickled, he jumped up and started screaming as he ripped his shirt open to see what was inside. The snake fell out of his shirt and started to slither away. Realizing it was a snake, he began jumping up and down trying to get away from it, which woke everybody else up. By now, Professor Jones woke up with at start and happened to look down. Seeing a snake coiled up on his belly, he jumped up quickly as well, cussing at the snake. Now both men were jumping up and down, screaming. From a distance it looked as if there was some kind of war dance going on around the fire with the two men carrying on so. The good news was the snakes got away without being hurt and the two men were now fully awake and would be the rest of the night as they watched for more snakes trying to stay warm. Both of them were now looking all around on the ground and reacting to anything that remotely looked like a snake. Jim and Julie, looking at Professor Wainwright, smiled at each other, knowing it was going to be a long night for their two guests. With that, they went back to sleep while the other two basically kept guard all night, dozing in and out.

The next morning came early and bright for everybody at the camp. Professor Jones and Nesbitt were finally able to fall asleep sometime during the night and were still asleep when the other three woke up. Jim got up and put some more wood on the fire to get everybody warm from the morning chill. Professor Wainwright and Julie saw Jim motioning them to be quiet and follow him. Quietly, all three of them left the camp, leaving Nesbitt and Professor Jones asleep next to the fire. All of them moved up the trail towards Red Hawk, who was standing and waving at them to come up to where he was.

"Just out of curiosity, why did you take the man's shoes?" Jim asked Red Hawk.

"Running Bear liked his shoes and took them to see if they would fit him. They didn't, so he returned them to the man," Red Hawk replied.

Jim and Julie started laughing at the comment, as did Red Hawk. As they followed Red Hawk up the trail, they came into the camp that the Indians were using for their food and shelter. Red Hawk introduced the three other Indians sitting at the fire as Running Bear, Grey Cloud, and Big Eagle. All of them tipped their hats as he introduced them to the team. Jim introduced Julie and Professor Wainwright to the four Indians. Big Eagle asked, "Is anybody hungry, we have some fresh-killed possum strips mixed with buzzard eggs ready to eat."

Red Hawk started laughing, "Don't you believe him; it's bacon with some eggs mixed together."

The others laughed at Big Eagle, who said, "What, I was only trying to be an authentic Indian."

Jim looked at Julie, who was now smiling, and the Professor, who was ready to eat about anything. As they sat down, Red Hawk asked, "So what do you want to do with the other two down there?"

"I'm not quite sure yet. Let me have some time to discuss it with my friends here."

"As you wish."

"Well, what do you want to do about our sleeping beauties down the trail?" Jim asked Professor Wainwright and Julie.

"Is there a way we could leave them up here for a while?" Julie asked.

"Do you think it would be all right if we let the wolves eat them?" the Professor asked.

"You know, that's a good idea, Professor. One thing for sure, if they get down off this mountain they won't leave us alone till they have the gold and possibly one of us getting hurt in the process," Jim replied.

"We can't kill them, but we can't let them go, either," the Professor said.

"How about we let Red Hawk and his friends take care of them," Julie said.

"I'm afraid we won't see them again if we do that. But, under the circumstances, I see that there is no other way to handle this," Jim replied.

All in agreement, Jim went back to Red Hawk. "Can you scare these two guys so bad that they won't want to come back looking for any treasure cave?"

"Your wish is our command, my friend. You stay up here and have some breakfast. This won't take long."

With that, the four Indian braves put their plates of food down, got up and went back down to where Professor Jones and Nesbitt were sleeping. This time the four braves were dressed in the old Indian wardrobe: buckskins and war paint with spears and bows and arrows. Red Hawk and Grey Cloud stood over the Professor while Big Eagle and Running Bear stood over Nesbitt.

Gently touching Professor Jones with the tip of his spear, Red Hawk called to him, "Wakey, wakey, Professor; it's time to wake up."

The Professor woke up and, seeing Red Hawk and his confederates dressed in traditional garb standing over them, he let out with a scream, which woke up Nesbitt. As both of them sat there next to the fire, scared and surprised, Red Hawk spoke quietly, "Do you want to live?"

Both of the men shook their heads yes. Red Hawk instructed, "Then leave this mountain and never come back. If you do come back, we will find you and kill you."

Summoning up all his courage, Jones stood up and screamed, "I want the treasure in the cave!"

With that, a bolt of lightning hit the ground in front of the Professor, knocking him to the ground. As the Professor lay face down, Running Bear came running over and, grabbing the Professor by the hair of his head and pulling his head back, he pulled his knife out and put it to the Professor's throat while he had his knee in his back. Red Hawk looked at the Professor, who was scared by what had just occurred, and repeated the warning again.

By now Nesbitt, who had seen what happened to the Professor, had gotten up and was running down the mountain trail with two of the braves whooping and hollering as they chased him. He didn't stop until he was near the truck, and only then to catch his breath. As he was leaning against the truck catching his breath, he found, as he checked his pockets, that he didn't have the key to either one of the vehicles. Looking around for the Indians that were chasing him, not knowing where they were, he decided to hell with waiting for the Professor, and kept on running down the road. After a while he was limping more than running because his feet hurt, and his legs ached from running the three hours back to the camp; nevertheless, he kept hobbling down the road to get away.

Both the Indian braves were laughing as they made their way back to the camp where Professor Jones was, talking about how scared the white man was. "He should make the Utah border by tomorrow noon."

The two Indians were now standing next to Red Hawk and were no longer smiling as he talked to Professor Jones.

"The decision is yours as to how this will turn out for you," Red Hawk said as he looked at Professor Jones, with his hand in the air to signal Running Bear.

Professor Jones, seeing that it all depended on him as to whether he lived or died on the mountain with Red Hawk waiting to give the order, he thought about what was happening and finally said, "Okay, you win. I will leave the mountain and will never return."

Red Hawk lowered his hand and Running Bear let go of his hair, getting up off the Professor's back. Running Bear stood there waiting to see what would happen next. The Professor picked himself up off the ground, mad at being beat at his own game. He started yelling at Red Hawk, cursing him and getting louder and more physical with each threat. This time the lightning hit the Professor, stopping him mid-sentence. Being knocked back about twenty feet, the Professor stood up, having been knocked senseless again, with his clothes smoking from the lightning strike, unable to speak or hear.

Running Bear went to him and, as he drew his knife again, the Professor seeing the Indian coming towards him took off down the trail heading in the same direction Nesbitt had gone. He was slipping and falling while trying to keep moving down the trail. Red Hawk followed him, yelling to the Professor, who was now running scared, "Remember what I told you."

The Professor ran all the way down the trail and was at the base camp in short time. Finding his keys and getting into the truck, he drove out of the Gorge area, almost hitting Nesbitt as he came around a curve on the dirt road, stopping only once to pick him up as he was still half running, half limping down the road. Realizing it was the Professor driving the truck, Nesbitt stopped long enough to climb into the truck, so they could continue making their way back to Utah. The Professor was now just starting to be able speak again. The ringing in his ears would be there until he got home.

As Jim was sitting and having some breakfast with Julie and Professor Wainwright, he could hear Red Hawk laughing with the others as they made their way back to their camp. Red Hawk, looking at Jim, said, "I don't think the Professor will be a problem for you anymore."

"What did you do to them?" Julie asked.

"You really want to know? Well, we scared them pretty good. In fact, Nesbitt took off running down the trail before the Professor did. The Professor was harder to convince, but he finally got the message, as well, after we gave him a couple of near-death experiences to get his attention and threatened to scalp him."

Jim thanked Red Hawk. "We couldn't have done it on our own back there. Those two men were ready to kill for the treasure in the cave and would have done it if you guys hadn't been there to stop them."

"Oh, we were just having some fun with them. Thank you for letting us do it," Running Bear said, as he sat down picking up his plate to have some more breakfast.

After breakfast was done and everybody was getting ready to go back down the mountain, Red Hawk called Jim over. "Do you want to see something that is really interesting and kind of what you've been looking for?"

"Yes, I would like that very much."

"After breakfast I'll show you some things that will make you stop and think about archeology in a totally different way."

Jim, looking at him, wondered what he meant and was anxious to see what lay ahead further down the trail.

Chapter XIV

When everyone was done with breakfast and had all their gear packed and ready to go, Jim nodded towards Red Hawk and said to Julie and her father: "Before we head back down the mountain, Red Hawk has asked me if I would be interested in seeing something new and unusual that very few people have seen. The scientist in me couldn't say no and I thought you guys might be interested in it as well. What do you think?"

Julie and the Professor were now curious as to what Red Hawk wanted to show them. Both nodded yes to Jim's question and now were eager to see what Red Hawk was talking about.

At this point Jim looked at Red Hawk. "Lead the way."

As they continued following the trail on top of the mountain, Red Hawk was watching the three of them. Running Bear came up to Red Hawk, asking, "How do you think they'll handle what they see?"

"I think they'll do just fine after they get used to the idea of what they are looking at."

"The question is, how long will it take for them to get used to it."

"Yeah, I know what you mean, hopefully not too long."

After two more hours on the trail as they headed down the mountain, Jim asked Red Hawk, "Would it be all right to take a five-minute break to catch our breath?"

Red Hawk stopped and sat down on a rock and patiently waited for the three of them to catch their breath. "It isn't far now. We're almost there."

"That's good," said the Professor, "I'm afraid I'm not as young as I used to be for climbing and hiking in the mountains. I'm afraid I'm getting old."

"You're doing fine, Dad. I want you to know I'm tired too," Julie said.

Jim, taking some water from his canteen, drank deeply from it. Looking around, he noticed that the trees were turning back into scrub oak instead of the pines that they had been in at breakfast time. Jim also noticed that there were more rock outcroppings; in fact, it reminded him of some of the areas in Utah around the central part, close to Manti and Salina. Jim realized that he had never been in this area of the Gorge, and as he was looking at an area he hadn't expected to see this kind of terrain in this part of Colorado. As he continued looking the area over, he could see some big rock formations off to his right. "Are we headed in the direction of those rock formations?" he asked Red Hawk.

"Yes, we are. We will find some interesting petroglyphs over there along some of the walls in the valley."

When everyone was rested again, they continued to make their way to the rock formations off in the distance. As they got closer, the rock formations were actually quite large, and all of them could see how beautiful the area was. All around they could see places where there were caves and openings suggesting possible places of habitation. As Red Hawk slowed down, he waited for Jim, Julie, and the Professor to get closer to him. Stopping when they got near him, he said, smiling, "Follow me, but be very careful as you climb this rock."

As they made their way up the rock, Jim helped Julie and the Professor get on top of it. The rock itself was more like a big boulder that was large enough to block a two-lane road. Standing on top of the boulder, the whole panorama opened to them to show a valley of huge mountains and rocks. On one side was a cliff that was steep and about one thousand feet tall and about three thousand feet long, somewhat similar to Mesa Verde, except larger. Red Hawk let the view soak in for his guests and then, pointing out the other side of the canyon, he said, "See the other side over there."

Again, as they looked at where he was pointing, they could see another cliff face and this one bigger than the one on the other side of the valley. Jim couldn't believe his eyes, and the Professor just stood there looking at the whole area, trying to figure it all out. Looking on the valley, he asked, "Is this a city of some sort?"

"Yes, this is our city that we grew up in many years ago. Our home is on that side of the valley over there," Big Eagle said.

"Running Bear and I live on the other side of the valley about midway up the face of the cliff," Red Hawk said.

Jim took his field glasses out and started scanning the rock cliffs from one side of the valley to the other. When he finished scanning the area, he brought his binoculars down and asked Red Hawk, "What does Big Eagle mean, many years ago?"

Looking around, he realized there was nobody else on the rock except him, Julie, and the Professor. Wondering what happened, he tried to find the four Indians, realizing they were not to be found anywhere. Confused, he looked at the Professor and Julie. "Did you see where Red Hawk went?"

"Who are you talking about? We followed you because you said you wanted to look at one more place before we left," Julie replied.

Jim was stunned that Red Hawk and the others with him had only been seen by him. Thinking for a minute, he then asked, "Professor Jones and Nesbitt, what happened to them?"

"They got scared off by a big bear that suddenly appeared at our camp near the waterfall," Professor Wainwright said.

"Are you feeling all right, Jim?" Julie asked.

"I'm not sure if I am. Well, let's get down off this rock and do some exploring. I've a feeling we might find something out here."

As they made their way towards the cliffs on the one side of the valley, Jim pointed out that there had been Indians living in this valley a long time ago. As they got closer to that side of the valley, the Professor spotted some petroglyphs near the base of the cliff, which ran the whole distance of the wall face. They depicted hunting scenes with the men riding horses, chasing what looked like elephants and deer. Another scene showed battles that had been won against a smaller but more numerous people. As they walked down the face of the cliff, they found a picture that showed another battle against what looked like giants, with smaller people being more numerous than the giants. The Professor started studying the glyphs, taking pictures of them while Jim and Julie went about looking for a way to get up and look at the caves in the face of the cliff. Jim was able to locate some stairsteps that led upward near the base of the cliff and slowly started to climb them. Julie followed behind him, making sure she used the same steps Jim had found. Within an hour they were standing on the first level of the cliff, looking into a small cave entrance. Using their flashlights, they found a mound piled up not far away from the entrance. Crawling through the opening of the cave, they found a room that opened into a large cave. Inside the cave was a rock table in the center of the room and stone boxes on the sides of the cave. One of the stone boxes looked like it was about three feet wide and about three feet long and was high enough that a person sitting down could use it as a table. Opening the box, they found artifacts similar to what they had found inside the medicine man's cave. Julie went further back into the cave and called out, "Jim, you need to see this."

Jim closed the lid on the box he was looking at and walked back to the area where Julie was standing. As he walked in he could see one long stone box on each side of the room they were standing in. Each box was about four feet wide and about ten feet long. Looking at Julie, Jim asked, "What do you make of these?"

"I think this is a burial chamber and these are the coffins where they buried people."

"This whole cave must be a sepulcher then," Jim said, as he thought about what Julie had said.

Using his light, Jim scanned the room, finding nothing except the tombs. Now turning his attention to the walls of the cave, he noticed that the walls had petroglyphs on them indicating battles, with two people in headdresses, one male and one female, being in the front, carrying weapons into each battle. On the other wall of the cave there was another picture of the same people hunting.

Being curious, Jim went over and tried to open one of the coffins in the room. With Julie's help they were able to move the top off one of them. Using their flashlights, they looked inside the coffin and found a man's body about nine feet tall, wearing a headdress with red hair protruding from it, plus all sorts of copper and gold plates as well. Looking back at the pictures on the wall, they could see one of the characters was wearing the same kind of headdress that they had found inside the coffin. Moving the lid some more, they were able to see that he was dressed in a royal cloak with his hands crossed on his chest. Moving to the other coffin, they removed the cover from it and, looking inside, they could tell it was a woman who stood about eight feet, six inches tall, fully dressed as well. She had blond hair that protruded from her headdress. Her hands were across her chest just the like the man had his. Inside her coffin were small containers of wheat all around the base. She had some kind of ceremonial cloak on as well, that was held together by two copper plates on her shoulders that were attached to her dress. Looking at the wall around her coffin, they saw drawings depicting a woman wearing a headdress, fighting in battle as well, and showing children around her. Both Jim and Julie had heard stories about giants who roamed the earth three thousand years ago, but they had only scoffed at the idea, thinking that somebody so huge had to be some kind of hoax. Yet here they were, inside a burial chamber with the remains of giants in their coffins. Taking pictures of everything and replacing the lids on the coffins, they left the chamber and went out to see the rest of the place.

As they walked around some more on the first level, Jim could see a lot of cave openings. Searching a few of them, he found the caves to be pretty much the same way. Each of them had a main room and then another room in the back with coffins in them. Finding the stairs once more, they climbed up to the next level. These caves were different from the first level. They were larger and bigger inside, and they looked more like living quarters, with fire pits in the center of the room for a whole group of people. This area of the cliff was big enough for a whole city to live here. Yet each place had a smaller area with a stone table in it.

Again, finding the stairsteps, they went to the next and final level. This area was bigger in size as far as rooms went; however, there were not as many rooms, actually only three. In each room, there were what looked like sitting stones, in rows. On one side of the room there was an opening, which allowed the sun to shine through, and there were more Indian paintings on the far wall, opposite the opening for the sun. The paintings showed a great big bear below the sun, and below him were other animals. There was also a picture of a tower with a bear walking away from it, leading people. These people, who now populated the earth, looked as if they had traveled from far across the sea in some kind of submarine-like boat. In one of the other pictures it showed a group of people living on the earth, but who appeared more like spirits, fleeing from the sun god to another world. Moving on to the next room, they saw it had not only paintings of animals, but the humans were dressed differently, worshipping the sun god and one other person standing next to the sun god. The third room they looked at had the sun god, who was seated, and one other person next to him, who was standing wielding a sword and fighting against a snake god and his horde and further down a large group of people that were fleeing to another place. There were no other humans in the paintings of this room, just the sun god and the person next to him, each having a white beard and fair complexion. Jim and Julie continued to take pictures as they went into the different rooms. Off this particular room was what looked like living quarters for one person.

By now the Professor was calling out to them, wondering where they had gone off to. Sticking their heads out and calling back, they made their way back down the face of the cliff to meet the Professor. Jim and Julie told him what they had seen on each of the levels they had been in. The Professor wanted to see for himself these giants that Julie and Jim had told him about. Climbing back up to the first level, Jim took the Professor with him through the first cave entrance, with Julie following behind her dad. Jim and Julie opened one of the coffins and the Professor couldn't believe his eyes. He too had heard of these giants but had never seen one before, except only in pictures. He stood there looking at the body of a man lying in his final resting place. Jim then opened the other coffin and showed him the woman inside it. Each of them looked regal in their attire as they rested in the coffins. After seeing the giants, the Professor asked, "Did you happen to notice they had six fingers and six toes on their hands and feet?"

Jim and Julie went back and looked again. Seeing what the Professor had noticed was true, this new-found information surprised them both. Jim thought aloud, "Why would that be the norm for these people?"

As they closed the coffins and walked out of the opening to the room back into the sunlight, all of them were trying to come to some kind of understanding of what they had seen. Not sure of where to go in his thinking, Jim said, "It looks to me as if the first level is for burials, the second is for the normal day-to-day living, and the third is for religious purposes only.

Climbing back down the stairs, they decided to go explore the other side of the valley. When they reached the other side of the valley, they noticed that the face of the cliff was clean, having no petroglyphs on it. Again, finding the stairsteps, they climbed up into the first level and found caves with living quarters and extra rooms. Each cave looked like a separate living area for one family. There must have been at least forty caves located on this level.

Climbing up to the next level, they found it was the same as the first level but with more separate living places for about thirty families. The third level was the same as the third level on the other side of the valley, with the exception of the rooms being smaller and not completely covered in paintings. These paintings showed the sun god standing with symbols emanating from him, with a tree of life below him that had water running from it in three different directions in the center of the wall. The tree seemed to be the main point in the picture and showed a group of people in single file making their way to the tree. Next to the trail was a dark area that was blackened with charcoal.

Jim, Julie, and the Professor were now trying to understand what they were looking at. Jim threw out his idea first. "What I find interesting is that the sun god is white and the people in the pictures are white too. The pictures on the third level on the other side of the valley show a white sun god, and the worshippers in the paintings are white as well. Both sides of the valley have a place where they worshipped, so it's obvious that they were a religious people. From what I remember from my studies, there is no history of white people being here before the Indians showed up, except in the Book of Mormon."

"And as of yet, nothing has been found to prove or disprove the Book of Mormon is true from an archeological perspective," the Professor said.

None of the others could understand the pictures they had seen in the religious areas of the valley. Moving on in their conversation, Julie noted, "It looks as if the first two levels were for living day-to-day lives. The third level was the same as the other side of the valley, a religious area."

Jim added, "Maybe the second level on the other side of the valley was for businesses to buy and sell their wares to support the people for food and other things they needed to live. This side of the valley could be for only daily living."

"It looks as if the center of town was on the other side of the valley, where they may have posted the latest news about hunting expeditions and the latest news about battles and such. I think what we have here is a complete city inside this valley," the Professor said.

"That is the same impression I get as well. The thing that blows my mind is that the third level on both sides of the valley shows a battle involving the sun god and one other person against many people. It shows something emanating from the sun god and forcing their common enemy to flee from their presence to the earth. You can see the same kind of people in the first room," Jim concurred.

As they continued talking, the sun was making itself known by starting to sink into the western sky. They all wanted to stay but, not having the proper equipment, they decided to leave the valley and head back to the waterfall to camp. Climbing back up the mountain, they followed the trail that brought them. This time it would be a little slower due to the fading light. Looking back one last time before the valley disappeared behind them, Jim and the others didn't say a word as they continued their climb up the mountain.

It was past dark when they found themselves by the waterfall once more. Finding some wood, they restarted the fire and, eating the last of their cold food, they retired for the night, sleeping in the same places they had the night before.

As they slept, Jim had a dream and in it he saw Red hawk and his three companions. They were smiling at him but not saying a word. Jim tried to understand why they were smiling, and after a couple of minutes he figured it out. They were pleased to show off their valley, and the things Jim, Julie, and the Professor had figured out were correct. In the dream Jim could see the place come alive with the people living there. They were giants and they had thrived there for many years. In one scene he saw the battles that had raged between them and another group of giants. Each time, Red Hawk's group came off the conquerors, and Jim could see the people were blessed by the Great Spirit for their belief in him.

Jim now was awake and listening to the waterfall. As he lay there he tried to imagine what it would be like to have lived among the giants during that time. He could only wonder what it would have been like to be part of this way of life, with all their trials and triumphs. Closing his eyes once more, he fell asleep. This time the dreams were gone.

Chapter XV

When the sun rose the next morning, Jim was still asleep and didn't want to move from his bed of pine boughs, simply because he was warm, and the morning chill was just starting to be felt. Julie was the first to wake up and she reached over to kiss him. This caused him to smile and, opening his eyes, he saw Julie next to him and he returned her kiss with his own kiss. Jim looked at Julie. "When we get back to civilization, why don't we get married so we can do this every morning?"

"I thought you wanted to wait until we got our doctorates finished," she said in a surprised tone.

"I know what I said; I just feel that after everything that has happened lately I don't want to wait anymore."

"Are you sure?"

"Did you notice that in the valley families seemed to matter the most to these people, especially as to their religion? The impression I got was life is too short to be bothered with titles and such that can only be accomplished with a little more time. Loving you and having you raise our children and being a family is more important than all of the labels one can achieve in this world."

"Well, if that's how you feel, then I accept your offer and ask what took you so long?"

"It's a man thing. As the old saying goes, 'I'm a man and I can change, if I *have* to.'"

Julie, looking around the camp, found her father still asleep and went over to wake him up with the good news. Upon hearing this he said, "My boy, what took you so long?"

"Am I the only one that everybody was waiting for on this marriage thing?"

Both Julie and the Professor looked at Jim and started laughing as they shook their heads yes. Jim just sat there for a moment not saying a word except, "Maybe next time I'll be quicker in my actions."

"What do you mean *next time*; there better not be a *next time* for you, mister Jim!"

As they gathered their gear together, they put their backpacks on and headed down the trail that would lead them back to their vehicle and out of the Royal Gorge park. The hike out wasn't too bad, as it was all downhill, and they made good time getting to their vehicle. Getting in the Jeep, they were relieved to see it was still in one piece. They drove back towards Salida, stopping for breakfast and then on to find a motel to get cleaned up in. All three of them were famished and ate more than they should have of the pancakes and eggs, with plenty of juice to drink. Afterwards they went into the local Wal-Mart and bought some new clothes, so they could have clean clothes to wear. Once this was done they went back to the hotel room, where they each took showers to get rid of the smell of the campfire and get out of their camping clothes that they had worn for the last three days. They put their dirty clothes in a plastic bag for the trip home.

Being clean and fat from eating too much breakfast, they got back into their Jeep and headed west to Provo. As they pulled out of Salida they didn't see Professor Jones and Nesbitt sitting in the truck in the parking lot, waiting as they passed by them on the road. The scare that the two men had experienced had now worn off and now they were mad as all get out for all that had happened to them. Pulling onto the road behind them, they followed Jim and the others out of Salida.

Jim was oblivious to Jones and Nesbitt following them in their truck. He was lost in his thoughts about their experiences down in the valley. For all of them it was bigger by far than anything they had experienced before in their lives, almost as big as finding the cave with the gold plates in it. Each of them were trying to wrap their minds around all the stories they had heard or read concerning giants, and it was going to take some time to figure it all out. Right now, it was time to go back home to Provo and take a few days off to relax a little.

The drive was uneventful and rather quiet up to the point when they pulled into Montrose for gas. Julie and the Professor went into the gas station to pick up something to drink for everybody. While Jim filled the gas tank he checked the oil and washed the windshield. Not paying much attention to his surroundings, he didn't see Nesbitt or Jones come up on him. Nesbitt stuck a pistol in his side. "You move, and I swear I'll shoot you."

Jim, being taken by surprise, hadn't expected anyone to move in on him at the gas station, especially Nesbitt and Jones. Then Jones walked up to him. "So we meet again, Jim."

By now, Professor Wainwright and Julie were coming out of the store with the drinks they had just bought. Noticing there were two men with Jim by the Jeep, the Professor stopped and told his daughter, "Go back into the store and call the cops *now*."

Seeing Professor Jones and the other man standing there with Jim, she went back into the store and, doing as she was told, called the cops. Dispatch answered, "What is your emergency?"

"There are two men, one of which has a gun, holding my fiancé and my father hostage in front of the Sinclair station!" Julie frantically answered.

"We'll dispatch a deputy to your location."

"Thank you," Julie gratefully replied.

After she hung up she continued to wait inside the store. As she watched from the window, she could see her dad as he was talking to Jones and Nesbitt. Deciding to move closer, she heard Jones ask, "Where's the girl?"

"She had to use the restroom; she'll be out shortly," the Professor said.

In the distance Jones and Nesbitt could hear a siren going off, and as it got closer to them they started to get a little jumpy. Looking around for the girl, Jones decided not to wait for her. He ordered Jim and the Professor to get into the Jeep and start driving. Jim did as he was told, with Wainwright in the front passenger seat. Both Jim and the Professor had been surprised to be seeing Jones and Nesbitt so soon after being up on the mountain.

Driving out of the gas station and going back in the direction they had just come from, they headed towards Salida, on the state highway. The squad car pulled to a stop in front of the gas station, and the deputy jumped out with his gun drawn, looking for anything suspicious. By now Julie came out of the store, yelling, "They went back down the road in that direction!"

"Who are you?" the deputy asked.

"I'm the one that called you."

"Who are you; what's your name?"

"My name is Julie Wainwright, and they have my father and my fiancé in the red Jeep that just drove off."

"Where are you from?"

Julie couldn't believe it. The kidnappers were getting away while the deputy was asking stupid questions that could be answered once they caught up with the Jeep. By now Julie was mad at the deputy and started crying about her dad and Jim being kidnapped. The deputy tried to calm her down, but the frustration was real for her and she couldn't stop crying, saying one more time, "They are getting away!"

Jones and Nesbitt kept Jim driving down the state highway until they found a dirt road.

Ordering Jim to turn onto it, they kept going down the road until they were out of sight. Jones told Jim, "Stop the vehicle and turn off the engine," after he had found another place to turn off the dirt road.

Waiting for the squad car to drive by, they sat there for twenty minutes before deciding it was safe to go on down the dirt road again. After another ten minutes of driving, Jones had Jim stop the Jeep. Looking around, Jones figured he had driven far enough that they wouldn't be bothered by anybody driving by. Jones then told them to get out of the Jeep and said, "I guess you know why we're here, don't you?"

Jim, looking at Jones, said, "You missed us?"

Nesbitt took his gun and hit Jim in the back of the head with it. This time Nesbitt said, "You know you're really funny, you know that, don't you?"

As Jim picked himself up from the ground, he punched Nesbitt in the groin, "I thought I was; didn't you think so, Professor Wainwright?"

Nesbitt dropped his gun as he folded up and fell to the ground from the punch. Professor Wainwright picked up the gun and fired it into the ground until he thought the gun was empty. Jim picked up Nesbitt by the scruff of the neck and hit him with his fist, breaking his nose in the process. Jones just stood there and watched as Jim continued to beat Nesbitt into the ground. As Nesbitt lay there on the ground trying to recover from the beating, Jim said to Jones, "You were saying?"

Jones, looking at Nesbitt on the ground, realized that things had changed, and he wasn't in control anymore. He started backing up when Professor Wainwright fired the gun one more time and yelled, "Don't even think about running away, Jones!"

Jones, unsure of what to do, stood there waiting as Jim came over and punched him in the face. Jones went down to his knees and Jim, raising him up again, hit him one more time. This time, however, when Jones stood up after being hit, he threw dirt in Jim's face and then hit him in the stomach. Jim fell back, landing against the Jeep, and he shook his head to get the dirt out of his face and eyes. Catching his breath, he reached again for Jones, stepping into his punch to avoid being hit, and kicked him square in the groin. Jones went down, and Jim caught him as he fell to the ground. Taking Jones' head by the hair, Jim slammed it into his knee. This time Jones went down and stayed down as he laid there, groaning in pain. After a few minutes of resting, Jim grabbed Jones once more and dragged him over to where Nesbitt was lying on the ground and dropped Jones on top of him. Standing there for a moment looking at the two of them, he made his way over to the Jeep. The Professor came over as Jim was leaning up against the Jeep and took him by the arm and helped him stand until he got his balance again. The Professor took Jim to the passenger side of the Jeep, and Jim got in and sat there while the Professor got in at the driver's side and drove back to town to pick up Julie.

Going back to the gas station and looking for Julie, they couldn't find her. Asking the clerk inside the store about the young lady who had called the cops, the clerk said, "She went with the deputy down to the sheriff's office."

Getting the directions to the sheriff's office from the clerk, the Professor drove to the sheriff's station and found Julie sitting in the office while the deputy was filling out the paperwork. Julie, seeing her dad standing there, got up and ran to him, hugging him as she was crying. "I was so worried about you and Jim. I thought I'd never see you again."

"Come on, let's go home and leave this popsicle stand," her dad said, as he surveyed the situation in the sheriff's office.

As the two of them left the sheriff's office, the deputy looked up just in time to see Julie leaving through the door. The deputy got up and ran to the door to catch up with her. "Do you still want to file a report?"

Julie turned and looked at the deputy and laughed at him as she got in the Jeep and they drove off. The deputy didn't know what to do and went and sat down at his desk and continued to work on the report.

Seeing Jim safe and sound made things all right once more for Julie. The Professor proceeded to tell her, "Jim here is a real fighter. He kicked both Nesbitt and Jones' butts single-handedly and left them in a pile in the middle of a dirt road. You should have seen him!"

Julie, looking at Jim, was surprised by what her father had told her. "I have two brave men to protect me!" she said, smiling.

"Just don't expect it every time two men take us."

"Do you think they'll come after us again?" Julie asked.

"Hard to say, but knowing Professor Jones like I think I do, I would say there's a good possibility that we might run into them again. Just don't know where or when it will be," the Professor said.

"It may take them a little longer this time," said Julie. "While I was waiting at the Sinclair station for the sheriff's officers to arrive, I slashed two of the tires on their truck. Once they make it back into town they will need to buy some new tires."

"That won't happen till tomorrow morning when the stores open up again," Jim added.

"Gee, I didn't know you had such a mean streak in you, Jim," Julie said.

"Only when I get hit in the head by a bad guy."

"Well, remind me never to hit you in the head."

Chapter XVI

Driving the rest of the way home from Montrose, they arrived in Provo in the early morning. Unloading what equipment they had from the Jeep, they all found a place to sleep in the house and were out in minutes. Being able to sleep in their own beds was nice for Julie and the Professor. Jim slept on the couch as was his custom when he stayed overnight.

Later in the day, when the Professor was awake, he called the Dean at his house to let him know they were back and that he had some things that he wanted to talk to him about. Scheduling a time for the Dean to come over later in the evening, they agreed to a time of eight o'clock. In the meantime, the Professor would work on getting the pictures ready that they had taken of the valley while they were in Colorado. Jim, who was now up, aided the Professor in getting the pictures transferred onto a disc to give to the Dean as a backup copy for the school.

When finished with the disc, he ran the pictures through the computer to make sure everything would work correctly. By seven o'clock they were ready to show the Dean what they had seen in the valley and elsewhere. At eight o'clock the Dean rang the doorbell and the Professor, opening the door, invited the Dean in and offered him a seat in the front room. He proceeded to tell him of their experience being out in the field, finding the valley, and what they had encountered there.

The Dean sat back in his chair, listening to everything that was being said by the Professor, Jim, and Julie. He seemed surprised by what they had to say. After seeing the pictures of the valley, he was speechless. He had the Professor stop and leave the picture up on the screen when he saw the bodies of the man and woman in their coffins. Jim had put a dollar bill inside both coffins to give a reference as to the size of the skulls therein. When he saw the paintings on the walls inside the room where the coffins lay, the Dean was amazed at the similarities of the headdresses the man and woman inside the coffin wore to the paintings on the wall. He pointed out that the headdresses worn by the mummies in the caves and those worn by the local Indian tribes of the early west were very similar, thus proving there was a connection between the modern Indian 100 years ago to the giants that existed over 3,000 years earlier.

After the show and tell was done the Dean sat there in silence for a couple of minutes, taking everything in that he had seen and heard. The Professor looked at Jim and Julie, smiling, and then asked the Dean, "Well, what do you think about all of what we showed you?"

"When can you go back and do more exploring of this area?"

"When do you want us to go?" Jim asked.

The Dean looked at the Professor and then at Jim and Julie before speaking again. His voice was raised a little from being excited. "How about tomorrow, and this time I want to go with you to see this for myself. This is going to change all we know about archeology and the beginning of man. I really want to see this for myself Professor Wainwright. I want to be part of this find, not only for the university but to be part of something this big is awesome. I've waited all my life for something like this."

"You're more than welcome to go with us, Dean. I believe you should see this, as well, for yourself."

"All right, when can we leave to go back there?"

"How about in a couple of days, let's say, Saturday morning?"

"That will be fine. That way I can clear my calendar and be ready to go."

"I must warn you, Professor Jones is hot on our trail, trying to find the cave with the gold in it. He's kidnapped my daughter Julie once already and has tried to kidnap me and Jim on our way back to Provo this last time."

"I wondered what had happened to him since you left the last time from here. But, not to worry, he was let go for missing his class he was to be teaching for the last week. I have to tell you, I never really liked Professor Jones. I was always under the impression he wanted my job for his own and would do anything for it."

"I'm thinking you were right about him on that one, Dean."

"Well, let's call it a night and I'll see you guys Saturday morning about eight o'clock. Will that work for you guys?"

"Yes, and bring a sleeping bag, some extra clothing, and some food with you. I figure we'll be out there for about a week, maybe two."

"Will do, and good night."

"Good night, Dean."

As the Professor escorted the Dean to the front door, Jim and Julie looked at each other and smiled. Jim looked at the Professor when he came back into the living room. "It looks like the fun never ends for us this summer."

"I believe you're right. Now for you two to get ready for Saturday, you better hurry."

Both Julie and Jim looked confused at the Professor, wondering what he meant about hurrying to get things done. The Professor laughed, shaking his head, "You are planning on getting married, aren't you? I can't think of a better honeymoon than being in the middle of a valley in Colorado looking for giants, can you?"

Jim and Julie smiled and looked at each other, somewhat embarrassed by the Professor's comments and having forgotten all about it.

Jim, looking at Julie, said, "Well, what do you think, a honeymoon in Colorado under the stars in the middle of nowhere?"

"Sounds good to me, but I want a separate tent for us, if you don't mind," Julie said.

"Your wish is my command."

With that, the next morning Jim and Julie went to the Utah County Courthouse in Provo and filed for a marriage application and then went to the Justice of the Peace and got married. It wasn't exactly what they both had planned for, as weddings go, but due to the schedule and the work they were about to start, it would have to do till there was more time to plan. They spent their honeymoon the first couple of nights in the Radisson Hotel and enjoyed breakfast in bed and being together forever in sickness and in health….

By Saturday everybody was ready to go. The two vehicles were packed, gassed, and oiled, ready for the trip. The Dean was there, acting a like college kid on his first outing into the field to do a dig. His enthusiasm was contagious to everybody on the team, and pretty soon all were anxious to be on the road for the next adventure.

The Dean and Professor Wainwright rode together in the truck, and Jim and Julie rode in the Jeep, each listening to their own style of music as they traveled down the highway towards the Spanish Fork turnoff and then turning towards Price. They had CB radios that they could use to talk to each other in case anything happened, making it easier for the drive this time.

As they pulled out of Price on the 191 route, they drove through to Green River, connecting to Interstate 70, from there it would be a straight shot to the next big city of Grand Junction, Colorado, a 240-mile trip that would take about four hours to drive. From Grand Junction to

Salida it would be another 180 miles, adding another three hours.

The team would spend the night in Salida, with one more hour to the entrance to Royal Gorge. Tonight would be the last night they would sleep comfortably before heading into the back country of Colorado. Getting two rooms for themselves, they met at six o'clock to eat dinner at one of the local restaurants in town. They picked a seafood restaurant to eat at called Currents, located on Main Street in Salida. This night they had live music playing so Jim and Julie took advantage of that and danced till their food was brought over to eat. The conversation topic of the night was all about what they hoped to find when they got to the valley and what to expect when they got there. The night life in the restaurant was lively and fun, which for the next day would be good for the sendoff.

Having an early breakfast at the Patio Pancake Place before leaving Salida, everyone was ready and anxious for the last leg of their journey to start. Getting back into their vehicles, they drove through Salida to the Royal Gorge Canyon and park. The country was considered high desert with scrub pine and big rocks all around the area. The Dean studied the terrain as the Professor drove, commenting, "It's amazing that anything could survive in this kind of country and yet thrive in it."

"I agree. I find it remarkable too that anything, let alone human beings, could thrive in a place like this."

As Jim was driving he was looking around at the landscape of the high desert, as Julie dozed with her head on his shoulder. He had a feeling that this trip would be different. For whatever reason he wasn't sure, but something told him it would be different from the others that he had been on. He also felt it would turn out all right for everybody. Looking at Julie beside him, he realized he was a lucky man to have her in his life. He whispered to her, "I love you, sweetheart."

"I love you too," she mumbled back as she snuggled closer.

Within thirty minutes they took the turnoff to where their campsite was for their original dig. Stopping there to show the Dean what they had been working on for the summer took about twenty minutes. The Professor showed some of the areas where they had been digging on a map, also showing him where they had found the original cave where the medicine man was. The Dean seemed impressed with what he saw. "I believe you guys are the hardest working people I've ever met for this kind of archeological work."

"The hard part was keeping Jones and his lackey away from where we found the plates," said Wainwright, as Jim and Julie nodded in agreement.

The Dean led the way back to the vehicles, so they could go further up the dirt road that paralleled the Arkansas River. In about another ten minutes the Professor pulled off the road and onto a small turnaround, with Jim right behind him doing the same thing. From here, the rest of the way would be on foot, with everybody carrying their own supplies and food for the trip. "This is the trail we took to find the valley. From here it is all uphill," Jim said.

The Dean wasn't too excited about this part of the trek, but he knew what was waiting for them at the end of the trail, something that he had waited his lifetime to see and be part of. To him this was history in the making. It was decided that Jim would lead the way with Julie behind him, then the Dean following behind her, and the Professor trailing behind them all.

Jim, looking at his watch, noted it was nine o'clock, and the coolness of the morning air would feel good as they climbed the mountain following the trail. He figured it would be about five hours to make their way to the camp by the waterfall. They would spend their first night there and then move on from there to the valley. Talking this over with the Professor and the others, they all agreed with the plan. So off they went, hiking and climbing up the mountain and onto the ridge, looking for the river and waterfall.

Reaching the waterfall at about three o'clock, everybody was glad to stop for the night by the river. Both the Dean and the Professor were showing their age and were glad to have only this far to go for the day. Julie and Jim helped them both set up their camp before setting up their own. The Professor assisted the Dean in building the fire for the night, and they were ready to eat when Jim and Julie were done setting up their own camp. Cooking over the open fire, they enjoyed hot dogs and baked beans for their first night in the wilderness. Within an hour of eating, both the Dean and the Professor turned in for the night. Jim and Julie stayed up later to talk and watch the fire.

"So how are you doing?" Jim asked Julie.

"I'm doing fine, but I'm getting tired as well."

"Yeah, me too. It's been a busy day for all of us. I have to tell you, this trip is different than all the others that we've been on; leastwise, that's what I feel inside."

"How's that?"

"I'm not quite sure, but my gut is telling me to be careful and watch out for everybody on our team."

Julie, looking concerned, asked, "Be careful of what?"

"That's the problem, I don't know what it is to be careful of out here. There could be something out here that we have never dealt with before."

"What do you mean?"

"Well, for one thing, I'm the only one that saw the Indians the last time we were up here, and not having anyone else see them sounds like I'm crazy and maybe shouldn't be trusted to lead this group."

"But look where you led us. If it hadn't been for you, we wouldn't be back here to see it again. If you're crazy, It's all right with me. You just remember that I'm on your side, okay?"

Jim laughed. "You and your dad I trust, and the Dean as well; it's the unknown that has me concerned. Come on, let's go to bed. The fire will burn itself out."

As Jim lay there in his sleeping bag, looking through their tent, he could see the stars and the Milky Way as he was starting to get sleepy. Julie was already asleep, breathing gently as she lay next to him. Jim wondered what lay in store for them this time in the valley and cliffs that would be different. As he rolled over in his sleeping bag he thought to himself, *"Only time will tell."*

Chapter XVII

The next morning came too soon for everybody, as the day started off blustery and cold. Everybody stayed in their tents and in their sleeping bags for an extra hour till being forced to get up by their need to do their morning constitutional and to eat. Eventually, everybody gathered around the fire, trying to get warm as Jim put more wood on the fire. Once the fire was going briskly, breakfast could be started. Bacon and eggs with baked beans would be the first meal of the day. Julie started the process, with the Professor making some hot chocolate. The hot chocolate worked in getting everybody warm inside as they waited for breakfast. As everybody sat and ate breakfast, one by one they finished and started the teardown of the camp, putting their gear away and rolling up their sleeping bags so they could move on to the valley.

As they started their hike, all of them were still pretty excited about getting there. Jim and Julie were the first to be ready to go, and they began helping the other two to stow their gear and be ready to go as well. Making their way to the trail, they started hiking downhill into the valley. They continued following Jim, once again, as he took the lead. By nine o'clock the sun was shining and the cold of the morning was starting to dissipate as the grey clouds started to break. By noon the day was looking as if no storm had been in the area at all. The Professor pointed out the mountain to the Dean. "You see that over there?"

The Dean nodded his head as he looked at the mountain. "Is that where we are going?"

"Yes sir, we are. The best part is that it isn't too far from here."

"Good, I don't know how much more of this hiking I can do anymore."

The Professor smiled, "Dean, you've been behind a desk too long, you're doing fine."

"You know that desk never made me do exercises, either. Maybe I shouldn't have listened to it, I think," the Dean said as he continued hiking.

The Professor thought to himself as well, "*To be honest with myself, I don't think I can go any further, either. I'm definitely getting too old for this myself.*"

After being on the trail, Jim had everybody stop for their first break since leaving the waterfall. He and Julie sat down on a good-sized rock, catching their breath. Jim smiled, hearing the two Professors talk about being old, and commented to Julie, "I hate to say this, but sleeping on the ground has lost its appeal to me since waking up with a sore back."

"I don't understand, I slept well, considering you were my cushion," laughed Julie.

"Well, no wonder my back hurts!" chuckled Jim.

"And you were warm too," Julie snickered.

It had been an hour-and-a-half since breakfast, and they still had another hour to go to get to the valley. Then they could set up a base camp and start doing what archeology Professors do, and that is explore the area taking pictures and look for artifacts to catalog so they can verify dates and the location of what they are working on.

The Dean was still excited to see the valley. Although being somewhat tired, his desire to get to the valley kept him going. He knew there might be a treasure out there and that, as a kid, is what got him started wanting to be an archeologist, always searching for the buried treasure that somehow was just over the next hill or the next mountain. He had been doing this for quite some time and the fascination of looking for the treasure never went away for him. And so far, it had paid off for him quite well. Becoming a Dean at a leading university was quite an accomplishment, along with hunting for treasure, which he would have done no matter his station in life. Still, in all, the desire to find the golden treasure was always a constant drive within him, which for today was enough to overcome the tiredness he felt in his legs and body.

Reaching the boulder where Red Hawk had taken them the first time, Jim and the Professor helped the Dean onto the rock so that he could see the whole valley below him. Using his eyes that had been trained for years to look for anything like caves and signs that something human and old had been there, he took it all in, surprised at the vastness of the area that lay before him. At this point, the Professor said, "Now comes what you have waiting for and why you hiked up and down the mountain."

The Dean was speechless as he continued to look at the valley. "I've never seen anything like this before. It's just like you said. I had my doubts that anything could be as grand as you had described. I owe you an apology for not believing you."

"Apology accepted, Dean."

Jim explained to the Dean the layout of the valley from the rock and indicated where the tombs were and where most of the people had lived, pointing to the other side of the valley. The Dean took it all in, not saying a word.

"We need to be moving on to the valley now," Jim said as he started to climb down the rock.

Jim and Julie helped both the Professor and the Dean down off the boulder. Jim asked the Professor, "Where do you want to set up our camp while we're here?"

"How about we put it close to where we will be doing most our work."

"Makes sense to me," Jim said as they headed to the side of the valley where the tombs were located.

Julie followed Jim, with the Professor and the Dean slowly bringing up the rear, talking to each other while the Professor pointed out different things along the way. The Dean was heard to say, "This kind of reminds me of the Valley of the Kings in Egypt, don't you think?"

"Yes, it does, but the good thing is that we won't have to dig to find them."

Far up on the hill Nesbitt, with field glasses, watched as the team of archeologists made their way to the one side of the valley. Another man was standing next to him as he continued to follow the team with his binoculars. They had been following the group for almost a week, staying hidden in the shadows, not wanting to be seen by anybody. Realizing that something was happening, they waited patiently to see where the archeologists would lead them to find out what was going on. Hoping that maybe Jim and the Professor would show them where the cave, with the gold in it, was. Professor Jones continued to follow the archeologists with his binoculars, and he could tell Jim and the Professor had found a hidden city of the ancients. This would be considered a major find in the world of archeology and would be reported as such to the credit of the university. Jim, Julie and Wainwright would also receive credit for having found it. This made Jones angry, knowing that he would lose out on all the notoriety from it.

Both men were sporting bruises and black eyes from the beating they had received from Jim. In fact, Nesbitt's nose was broken, and both of his eyes were still bruised from it. Jones winced as he smiled, as he watched the team cross the desert, his face still puffy with some teeth that were missing from his own beating that he had received from Jim. This time, what Jim had done to them would be paid back to him in spades. Carefully, the two men quickly made their way down the trail to go into the valley to see for themselves what had brought Jim and his cohorts here.

Staying on the opposite side of the valley, they moved with a determination to stay out of sight. Their hope was that Jim and the others would do all the work for them in finding the artifacts and treasures. Once it was all collected they would go in and take it right out from under their noses, then they would get all of the notoriety and credit for the discovery. They would leave Jim and the others in the desert in unmarked graves. Jones thought what a fitting place to never be seen from again, and no one would be the wiser for it.

Nesbitt continued to watch as Jim and his team started to climb up the face of the cliff as they looked for a place to set up their camp. Nesbitt was thinking about how to get rid of Jim, smiling and thinking of all the different ways it could be done. The best part of this plan was that no one would know where to look for them.

Jim and the Professor decided that, for all purposes, they could set up their camp on the second level, above the tombs. That way they would be safe from the wild animals and close to their work.

When camp was set up and everything was in order, the Professor took the Dean down to one of the tombs and showed him the coffins inside, opening each one of them. The Dean was able to see the remains of the giants that had been entombed there. He was silent as he looked at the bodies inside the coffins, noticing their crowns, the clothing they wore, and the other artifacts buried with them. As he stood there looking at them, the Professor said, "There are more of these in the other chambers on the first level. We never did count them all, but there are quite a few of them."

"This is amazing. Is there a chance that we can take any of them back with us to the university?"

"Unfortunately, no for two reasons: first of all, how would we get them out of here and, secondly, the other reason is that the Indian nation would consider it sacrilege to disturb them."

"Yes, I see your point on both counts, although we could learn so much more from them back at the university."

"I agree; however, the best we can do right now is to take pictures of each tomb and what's inside them, documenting everything for our records. It will have to be enough right now, considering all that we are able to accomplish without all of the proper equipment while we're here in the valley."

The Dean thought about all that the Professor had said, "As much as I would like to take one of these skeletons home, back to the university, I agree with you on what you say. The best we can do is prove it with pictures."

"We can take pictures of the plates as well and translate them later at the university. Besides, we are the only ones that know about this, and I'm not planning on telling anyone else about it."

"After dealing with Professor Jones, neither am I."

Julie came into the tomb where her dad was talking to the Dean. "Jim has found something that may be of interest to you guys. He told me to come and get you and have you come over when you get the chance."

"It just so happens we are ready, so lead the way," Professor Wainwright said.

Julie went out of the tomb first. "He's in the last one over here."

Arriving at the tomb where Jim was, they walked in as Jim was taking pictures of the body inside a coffin. When they walked in Jim said, "Take a look at this body, Professor."

The Professor raised the lantern in his hand over the body inside the tomb and stood there looking at it for a moment, then called the Dean over to take a look at the body. Both of them stared at the face of the mummy. The face showed two sets of teeth, with eight of those teeth being canine teeth used for tearing meat from the bones of the victims. The other outstanding feature was that his head was covered with red hair. Both Professors realized they were looking at something quite different from the other bodies in the other caves. The Professor lifted his lantern higher inside the tomb and looked at the walls. There on the walls were pictures of giants killing people and eating them. Jim watched the Professor and the Dean for their reactions to what they saw. The Professor walked over to one of the paintings and carefully studied it. Then moving slowly down the wall, he saw that the smaller people used fire to scare the giants away into a cave. The next picture showed a fire in the front of the cave and the giants inside it. The following picture showed the people dancing and the remains of the giants lying on the ground. Looking back at the Dean, who had been following him as he walked the wall with his light, the look on the Dean's face said it all. He could tell that the Dean was surprised by what he saw.

Jim and Julie waited for the Professor to speak before saying anything. The Professor, looking at Jim and Julie, now said, "I'm not sure what to make of this. "Is this the first of the giants that died, or could it be a survivor of the fire?"

"I think you may be right about the giant being a survivor, Professor, except when the Indians thought they had killed all of the giants, maybe they hadn't, and this one was captured later," Jim said.

"Maybe they settled here in the valley to keep away from the Indians," the Dean interjected.

"Evidently, more than one got away, if that's the case," Julie added.

Jim, still standing next to the coffin, said, "This one is different, not only in the teeth but in size as well. This one stands at least fifteen feet tall, which is taller than the first ones we found in the tomb that look like a king and queen."

The Professor, walking over to the coffin and looking at the bones of the giant, agreed with Jim that this one was taller and broader at the shoulders than the others they had found. This time, looking inside the coffin, there was none of the usual stuff left behind in it: no written plates, artifacts, breastplates, weapons, or anything that indicated a warrior, per se, or kingly position. This one giant was considered a "persona non grata."

Now looking around the cave, the Professor started to see that there were stacks of animal bones on the floor of the tomb. And walking back to the opening of the tomb, he saw some place holders for something that went across the face of the tomb on both sides of the opening. Studying the place holders, he said, "Take a look at these notches in the rock."

All of them gathered around, looking at the notches. The Professor began looking around the area outside the cave and found some long round poles near the opening, outside the cave. Picking one of them up, he placed it in the notches, and it fit perfectly. Taking the other poles, he continued to fill each of the notches until all of them were filled. Stepping back and looking at the poles in the notches, he looked at Jim. "I think what we have here is a cage for this giant to live in."

"I can imagine that this giant was wild and the only way they could take care of it was to lock it up and feed it, as you would an animal," the Dean said.

"But why would you keep him in a cage when it would have been easier to kill him and be done with it?" Julie asked.

Taking the poles down from the front of the cave, the Professor walked back into the tomb. Raising his lantern, this time looking at the other wall nearer the coffin he saw more paintings on the wall. The paintings showed a battle between the one set of giants and another set of giants. The one set of giants was being led by two people, male and female, who were wearing headdresses. They were carrying spears in one hand and swords in the other hand. The giants they were attacking were using clubs and rocks against them. As the Professor moved down the wall, he saw that there were more of the ones with the clubs than there were of the ones being led by the king and queen. The last picture showed all the giants with the clubs and rocks lying on the ground, with the exception of one giant. He had ropes attached to him with the other giants leading him into a cave with bars across it. The Professor looked at the others. "This giant was the survivor of a battle between the people of the valley and wherever these other giants originated. I would assume they were chased out of the area they had lived in and ended up fighting with the people of the valley and becoming extinct."

The Dean and the others, still looking at the paintings on the wall, could only guess that what the Professor had said was true.   Jim, looking at the Professor, said, "So what I gather is that there were two groups of giants living in the same area at the same time, with other people as well, namely the Indians."

"I think you are correct in your assumption, Jim."

"Man, this valley was sure crowded with people all over the place then," Julie said.

"You could say that, especially if the one set of giants were cannibals eating another set of human beings that lived here in the area.   I wonder if the people got tired of feeding them and decided to fight back like it was shown in the cave where the creatures were killed by fire," the Professor replied.

"Can you estimate how far back these people went timewise?" Jim asked.

"Based upon all of the artifacts that we've found so far, I'd say, as a rough guess, maybe three thousand years ago.   The one thing that is puzzling to me is that some of the artifacts that are here that I have looked at are more current timewise than some of the others that we have found and dated from other sites."

"Are you saying some of these artifacts are what we would consider modern- day timewise?" the Dean asked.

"Yes and no. What I'm saying is that some of the artifacts in the tombs go back three thousand years, and others that are on the level where we are camped are what I would consider modern age, like early American Indian."

"Are you saying that there are giants living here now?" Jim asked as he looked around.

"Well, think about it, how many sightings do we hear of when people claim they've seen Sasquatch, Yeti, Bigfoot, or Skunk Ape? I'm not saying that the giants are Bigfoot or Yeti or anything like that, but what if Bigfoot or Yeti could be giants with fur to protect them from the elements?"

As everybody thought about what the Professor was saying, he continued, "Don't get me wrong, I really don't know, and at this point I'm just talking. I have no proof of any of this conjecture; however, what if it was true? What if there was a connection between all of these sightings and this place and other places like it?"

Now everyone was silent and thinking about all that the Professor had added in the conversation. Seeing the sun was going down, they decided that, for now, it was time to go back to their base camp and kind of meander around the area first, looking at the artifacts that they had found, while there was still daylight.

For all of them, nothing had changed; but in all actuality, everything had changed, as far as their understanding of what they had been working on. Jim and Julie went off on their own to gather firewood and to be alone. The Professor was thinking about what he had said, while the Dean was looking around the area where they were camped, wondering if this place was still alive with people and things that they thought had passed away. What if there were giants still living in the area, like what they had seen in the paintings on the walls? Maybe they would find one or two of them while they were here in the valley. Maybe they were being watched right now and not even knowing it.

Jim and Julie, once they were alone, just held each other, not saying a word. Each of them was lost in their own thoughts and wondering if they were walking on hallowed ground, ground that had been fought over by giants, just like in the paintings in the caves. Picking up some firewood to keep the fire going for the night, they headed back to the base camp with their load of wood, still silent. Jim spoke first when they arrived. "It really is interesting to think that we think so one-dimensional. Here we are, thinking that all of these people had lived thousands of years ago, and yet the thought of them being alive never entered our minds. As archeologists, we see the world one way and think it's correct. The question is, who said so? In our vanity, we think we know it all and yet, once more, we are shown that we know nothing at all."

"Now you understand what it means to be educated and dumb at the same time," said the Professor. "We know so very little about anything when it comes to man being on the earth, and the best we can do is guestimate everything we know and hope it is right."

"The best we can hope for is that we may be right for parts of it, knowing we could be wrong on all of it. The more we find, the less we know," the Dean added.

"I guess this is what makes our jobs exciting and interesting, isn't it," Jim said.

"You got it, and that's the challenge of every scientist in any field of research," replied the Professor.

At this point the Dean said, "I don't know about you guys, but I'm hungry for dinner."

As Jim and Julie put the firewood down near the fire pit, the Dean worked to get the fire started. Julie pulled out all the fixings for dinner while Jim sat back and watched the Professor check the book he had been writing in. Once the fire was going strong, the meal of the evening would be hamburger and baked beans. As they sat there eating, the Dean said, "I've something to say in reference to our earlier conversation today. About twenty-five years ago, a rancher in Sanpete County, Utah, was looking for new ground for his cattle to feed on. As he was looking, he came across a cave and, being curious, he climbed down into it to check it out. Inside he found a room that looked like living quarters for someone, and as he continued to explore, he found another room in the back, off of the main room. Not seeing anything in that portion of the cave and not having enough light to see anything, he went back out of the cave to head home. Coming back the next day with a lantern and a shovel, he went down into the cave and started looking around the interior of it. As he continued to look, he found another room inside that was off of the main portion of the cave, so, in all, there were three rooms. Each room was set up differently, for each had a separate purpose. The second room held coffins inside it, whereas the first room was a sleeping area. The third main room was for writing on the gold plates that he had also found nearby. The main room had all of the tools necessary to work on the plates. The sleeping area had a rock bed in one of the corners. He went into the third room where the coffins were located and was able to remove the lids of the coffins. Inside he found gold and tin plates that had writing on them. The bodies inside the coffins were similar to what we have found here in this valley. The breastplate and other brass objects were basically the same as here. The main difference is that the Sanpete cave is closer to the university.

The rancher brought the plates to our school to see if they could be translated, which of course they could. The plates tell a story of a group of people who lived in the valley and called themselves Christians, and it describes the wars they had with their enemies. When it came time to retrieve the plates, the school asked if they could hold on to them for a while longer. After that, the plates went missing. The rancher continued to dig in the cave and found another set of bones that stood nine feet tall. The bones were buried in a deep hole in the ground inside the cave. Among some of the stuff the rancher found were writings on metal sheets made of lead, and some arrowheads and all sorts of artifacts used for living in the cave. In fact, in the 1980's, some workers putting up a fence found another cave just on the other side of the Manti Temple, and some more tablets were located inside it. They ended putting up a fence around it as a safety concern. Whatever was on the tablets no one knows to this day, as they were collected by the local church leaders and never seen again."

As everybody sat there listening to the Dean, the Professor asked, "How come I was never told about any of this?"

"The university president at that time, under the direction of the prophet of the church, decided a long time ago that it was too dangerous, for lack of a better word, to let the general public know about what had been found. They determined that someday in the future it would be allowed to come out."

"Who was going to decide when the time was right?" Jim asked.

The Dean shook his head. "I don't know the answer to that question."

"What ever happened to the rancher?" Julie asked.

"The rancher was treated like a fool by everybody in the area, including this school, by some of the Professors, because of what he claimed to have found, and he never really recovered from it. He became a recluse and continued working on the cave, digging and writing in his journal, till he died. As it turned out, he kept meticulous records on everything he found in the cave. Just before he died, he went back to the entrance of the cave where he had found all of the artifacts and the two coffins and, using a stick of dynamite, blew up the entrance, hoping that what he had found would be lost forever. And for the last twenty or thirty years no one has been able to find it. However, that being said, some have claimed they have found the original entrance, but they are being tight lipped about it as well. There are some who say that the west side of the canyon around Manti and Ephraim, is covered with these giants' bones, buried deep, and if you know what you're looking for and if you have the right equipment to use, you can find the burial sites. Until recently, there have been a lot of these giant bones found that are similar to what the rancher described. According to the Bible, Goliath was one of these giants, and he had some brothers as well. For more modern times, there is a story that's been circulating about one giant found back in the year of 2002 in Kandahar, who had been killed by some Special Forces soldiers looking for the Taliban."

"What about these other sites, where are they located?" Jim asked.

"All over the Mississippi Valley, all the way to Ohio and Michigan, and along the East Coast of the United States as well. Some have been found in California and Death Valley and even found in Payson, Utah, and now in Colorado, and that's not counting the ones they've found all over the world," replied the Dean.

"So, this isn't the first place that these kinds of bones have been found, that are this size?"

"These are the best I've ever seen, for being so old and intact. But, no, the problem is that when they're found they disappear as if they never existed."

"Where do they go and who gets them?"

"Some say the government gets them and stores them where they can't be found, kind of like the movie *Indiana Jones and the Search for the Ark and Covenant*. Others have claimed that the Smithsonian Museum dumped a bunch of them into the ocean years ago. However, that being said, no one really knows for sure."

"After all you've said, what do you believe, Dean?"

After thinking about the question, the Dean said, "I believe I'll have a cup of hot chocolate, if you don't mind."

Everybody smiled at his comment and knew that was the end of the conversation about what the Dean had to say. All of them decided that a cup of hot chocolate would be good for a nightcap.

Jim and Julie looked up into the sky watching the stars starting to appear and feeling the chill in the air. Julie drew closer to Jim, who seemed mesmerized and deep in thought by all the stories from today and around the fire tonight. Looking across the valley, he thought once more of the dream he had of the people he had seen living here. What would they think if they saw these people coming into the valley and their homes to review and dissect their lives for the purpose of science, he wondered. The Professor brought over some cups of hot chocolate for the two of them and stood there looking over the valley and the horizon where the stars met the land. "Isn't it amazing that tonight we are seeing the same sunset that the original people of the valley saw three thousand years ago."

Jim and Julie smiled at the Professor and Julie hugged her father. "What was that for?" asked the Professor.

"For you being you, Daddy."

After they had all finished dinner and drank their hot chocolate, they all turned in for the night, each crawling into their sleeping bag and soon thereafter turning out the lanterns. After about five minutes the full moon and the stars in the sky was all the light there was for them to see by.

Chapter XVIII

From their vantage point across the valley, they could see the lights go out at the base camp. Waiting a few more minutes, they made their way down the hill to the tombs on the first level. Walking in and then turning on their lights, they saw the coffins, and being quiet, they opened one of them to see what was inside. Professor Jones was surprised by what he found inside. The remains were larger than he had ever seen before anywhere. Nesbitt was impressed by what he saw as well. Taking pictures and then going over to the second coffin, they opened that one as well, seeing another body inside the coffin that was just as surprising as the first one. Professor Jones knew what this meant, not only from a scientific viewpoint but also a monetary one. He would be rich and famous for having the skeleton of a giant with him everywhere he chose to do a talk. People would pay to see this, and the museums would have to pay extra just to have it on display. Closing the coffins up once again, they went from place to place looking in each of the tombs, finding skeletons in each one of them. Jones started thinking he had hit the jackpot and all of the money would be his for all of the skeletons. The question that crossed his mind now was how to get rid of the Professor and the others, so he could claim the skeletons for himself? Looking at Nesbitt, he thought that he might come in handy, after all, as a solution to this problem.

They headed back across the valley up to the hill where they had started from. Both of them started to plan how to get rid of the others so they could get the skeletons and how to transport the skeletons out of the valley. Sitting in their cold camp, the two of them were feeling cold from the night air but were warm inside from the discovery of the tombs. They both had dollar bills dancing in their heads and great plans on what they were going to do with their share of the money.

"We could take them one by one or we could take them all at once," Jones said.

"It would be easier to take them out all at once; that way the surprise would be in our favor," Nesbitt said.

Jones agreed, "What do we do with the bodies afterwards?"

"We bury them in the desert on the other end of the valley. That way they will never be found."

"How do we get them to the other end of the valley?"

"We walk them there. Then we have them dig their own graves.

"That works for me. When do we want to do this?"

"Right after dinner tomorrow night, before sundown."

"Okay, that will work," Jones said, smiling, as he looked at his gun, pulling the clip out to make sure there were enough bullets in it.

As Nesbitt watched Professor Jones check his gun, he in turn checked his own gun and made sure that the safety was on, just in case the Professor had a change of mind about splitting the money. He thought to himself, "Once we get the skeletons out of the valley, that will be a good time to get rid of the Professor and sell the skeletons to a museum."

Professor Jones and Nesbitt, each having his own tent and sleeping bag, crawled inside, hoping to stay warm without a fire that might attract somebody's attention. As Jones laid there in his tent, he smiled, knowing what tomorrow would bring for him and his companion.

Tomorrow would be the last day for Jim, the Professor, the Dean, and Julie. Closing his eyes, he could hardly wait for it to begin.

The next morning was beautiful and pleasant with no clouds in the sky and a gentle breeze running through the canyon that could be felt at their campsite. Everybody seemed to be in good spirits and were ready to have breakfast to start the day. Julie started fixing breakfast and Jim went to find some more firewood with the Dean's help.

While they were scrounging for firewood on the valley floor, Jim saw some wood that would work well for their needs. Walking away from the Dean to get the wood, he went into a draw and as he made his way down the old riverbed, Red Hawk was waiting for him. Calling his name, Jim was startled by Red Hawk standing there. Red Hawk laughed at Jim for being so easy to scare. "You white people sure are a jumpy lot. I bet you're fun on Halloween night."

Jim, recovering from the scare, looked at Red Hawk and laughed. "It's a wonder we won the west at all."

"Who said you did?" Red Hawk said as he laughed.

"What can I do for you today?"

"Just to let you know that you had visitors last night, looking at the tombs. They have big ideas of what they want to do with the skeletons and the artifacts in the caves."

"Who was it?"

"Your old friends from the first trip. They mean to harm you and your friends."

"I wondered when they would show up. Where are they now?"

"Up on that hill over there. You want that me and brothers take care of them again?" Red Hawk asked as he pointed in the direction of the hill."

"Yes, I think that would be wise. They will not stop until somebody stops them for good and permanent."

"We can do that, my brother."

As Jim closed his eyes for a minute, Red Hawk was gone once again. This time, as he picked up the firewood, he looked for the Dean and finding him said, "I think we have enough firewood now. Let's get back to camp."

In five minutes the two of them were climbing up the face of the cliff back to the camp to deliver the firewood.

"What took you so long out there?" Julie asked them.

"I ran into one of my friends out there," Jim replied. Julie thought he was teasing and said nothing to his comment, except, "Time to eat, guys."

Breakfast would be eggs and bacon with baked beans as a side order. After breakfast Jim helped Julie with cleaning the dishes. Julie noticed that Jim had hardly said anything at all during breakfast and was really quiet, even while assisting in the cleaning. Julie, sensing something was wrong, asked, "Is everything all right, Jim?"

"Yes, everything is all right, just feeling jumpy is all," he said as he looked at her.

"Why are you feeling jumpy; what's going on, Jim?" asked Julie, concerned.

"Our old friends are back out there somewhere," Jim replied, pointing to the north end of the valley.

"You mean Professor Jones and his man are out there?"

"Yes ma'am, they are."

"Are you going to tell the others about it?"

"Yes, in fact, right now, if you'll finish drying the dishes."

Walking over to the Dean and the Professor and calling them together, Jim said, "Our old friends are out there on that hill over there."

The Professor, looking at Jim, said, "Man, they never quit, do they?"

"Evidently not, especially when it comes to making easy money."

"Who are you referring to?" the Dean asked.

"You know them already, at least one of them anyway, Professor Jones and his henchman."

"Professor Jones, I should've guessed it would be him out here."

"Well you guessed right, Dean," Jim replied.

"What do we do now that we know they're here in the valley?" asked the Dean.

"I think it would be wise to stay close to camp today and not wander off by yourselves unless you tell someone," Wainwright said.

"I agree with the Professor on this one. Julie and I will stick together and you two will be together. Wherever you go, try to let each of us know where you're going," Jim said.

"When do you think they will strike?"

"Hard to say. If I were them, I would do it later today, after we do some more work on the caves."

Professor Jones and Nesbitt, sitting on the hill, watched the team with their binoculars as they cleaned up from breakfast. Both were anxious to get going with their plans of getting rid of the Professor and his team. Again, the timing had to be right for this to work out correctly. Being patient in their waiting, they sat and played cards till it would be time to go. In the meantime, they would watch and track their movements with their binoculars.

Jim took Julie everywhere he went as he explained what the plan was about, not being separated without telling someone first. They went into one of the caves to do some more research on the plates they had found in one of the coffins. Julie was crying a little. Not wanting Jim to see this, she turned away from him. Jim, sensing something was wrong, put his arms around her. "Is everything all right?"

"I don't know, you tell me," she said, frustrated.

Jim, looking at her, saw the tears running down her cheek. "Everything is going to be all right. I need you to remain calm till this is done; can you do that?"

"I don't know if I can. I remember the last two times these guys were around. I don't want to lose any of you guys to these two greedy men, including *me*."

"I don't want to lose any of you, either, and I guarantee that it won't happen."

"How can you be so sure about that?" Julie asked as she looked into his eyes.

"I just am. You need to trust me on this," Jim said, knowing that if he told her about Red Hawk, that would be enough for her to think he was going nuts.

"Do I have a choice on this?" Julie said, laughing.

"No, not really, but I love you anyway."

At this point they started working inside the cave, annotating everything they found in it and its location in the cave.

The Professor and the Dean found themselves inside another cave doing the same thing, and both were enjoying being able to ply their trade together, finding new artifacts with each layer they removed from the floor of the cave as they pushed the dust and dirt away.

Chapter XIX

It was dinnertime by the time they were done playing in the caves and, again, dinner would be hamburgers with baked beans. At this time, the two men on the hill, having already climbed down the mountain, decided to make their play and came out in the open at the campsite. Climbing the stairsteps on the face of the cliff, they made their way up to the level where the team had their camp set up. Both had guns, and upon reaching the base camp they pulled them out to make their point. With their backs to the fire, none of the team heard the two men approach. Once they identified themselves, all of the team, seeing them standing there with their guns drawn, raised their hands in the air and stood quietly still. Professor Jones spoke first, "Well, well, well, it looks as if we got here in time for a bedtime story. We want to thank you for finding this place for us; we couldn't have done it without you."

"Did we interrupt you? Do please continue. We don't mean to intrude," Nesbitt said, smiling.

"What took you guys so long? We've been expecting you," Jim said.

"Shut up or I'll shoot you right now, smart mouth," Nesbitt said, as he pointed his gun at Jim's nose.

"Now, now, now, is that any way to talk to our benefactors? Well, we're here now, and we know what you've found, and it's going to make us rich. We want to thank you guys," Jones said.

"What are you going to do with us?" Wainwright asked.

"I want you to know that has been a real problem for us to resolve as well. In fact, my friend and I have had a big discussion all afternoon about what to do with you."

"What do you think we should do with you?" Nesbitt asked.

"Let us go," Julie said.

"Funny you should say that. In our discussion that wasn't one of the options we talked about," Jones replied.

"You don't know what you're messing with here. If you want to live, you should leave here now," Jim said.

Jones looked at Nesbitt and laughed, as he cocked the hammer on his gun. "Funny, I thought that was what we were supposed to say."

"You won't get away with this, you know. Eventually, people will find out," Wainwright said.

"But until then, we'll be rich. Now come on, we're wasting time, besides, who's going to tell them, you? I know we won't. Now move it or you can die here."

"Where are you taking us?" the Dean asked.

"We're going for a short walk across the valley, and don't forget your shovels."

"You go to hell," Jim said, realizing what they had in mind for them.

"Most assuredly we will, but until then, move! We, as you would say, are burning daylight."

Nesbitt went down the stairsteps first to cover them, as he watched Jim, Julie, the Dean, and Wainwright come down the steps. Jones was the last to come down.

"Man, you look terrible. What happened to you?" Jim said, looking at him.

About that time, Jones shot Jim in the leg, "The same thing that's going to happen to you."

Jim fell to one knee and Julie came rushing over to help him stand up. Jim was turning white from the pain, and shock was kicking in. Fortunately, the bullet passed through the leg, not hitting anything important or life-threatening to him. It would just hurt to walk on it till it healed.

Jones, looking at Jim, said, "I'm going to especially enjoy watching you die. I think you'll be the last to die; that way you can watch your friends and your new wife go first."

"Leave him alone. You've done enough," Julie yelled at Jones.

"Why, yes ma'am, I'll do that."

Nesbitt spoke at this point. "Can I have her for myself?"

"Why of course, what was I thinking? Please forgive me for thinking of only myself," Jones said.

Now Julie was going to be sick from just the thought of what they were talking about. Jim stood up, still feeling the effects of being shot. "You touch her, I'll kill you myself."

"But, Jim, you are in no condition to do anything. Shut up before I shoot you in the other leg as well and make your friends carry you to the place we have in mind for you," Nesbitt said.

The hike to the other end of the valley was about sixty minutes in duration and Jim felt every inch of the walk from the pain in his leg. Julie, with tears in her eyes, assisted him; but for all intents and purposes, it still hurt to walk.

As they made their way across the valley floor, Jim muttered to himself, *Red Hawk, where are you?*

It took them about another thirty minutes to find a proper site to start digging at the end of the valley. Jones and Nesbitt sat down on a rock. "Start digging and make sure it's big and deep enough for all of you. I don't want anybody to feel left out of this opportunity."

Jim did what he could to help dig the large hole, but most of the work was done by the others. The Professor watched as the sky grew cloudy and threatened rain. In fact, you could hear thunder in the distance. Jones yelled, "Keep digging; I don't want my friend and me to get wet out here."

In an hour Jones walked over to look at the hole. "That's good enough. We don't want the animals to have to dig too deep to get your bones, now do we?"

Lining every one of the team up in single file, in front of the freshly dug hole, Jones cocked his pistol and pointed it at the Dean. "You know, Dean, you're a real idiot. You should have stayed at the school."

By then, lightning struck the ground near Jones and Nesbitt. Both of them fell to the ground. Jim and the others fell into the freshly dug hole. Watching Jones and the man lying on the ground, not moving, the Professor grabbed one of the guns lying nearby. Out of the shadows came four giants dressed in warrior clothes, one of which was wearing a headdress that indicated he was the leader. He directed the other giants to pick up Jones and Nesbitt. Jones, recovering from the lightning strike, stood up and fired his gun at the leader, hitting him twice in the chest. The leader, who wasn't even phased by the shots, continued moving towards Jones. The giant, taking a hold of Jones, grabbed the gun, crushing Jones' hand in the process. Jones let out a scream of pain as the leader walked up to him and said, "What did I tell you the last time we met?"

Taking Jones by the head, he flipped him over his shoulder and threw him out into the desert. Jones landed in a clump of mesquite brush, not moving as he was dead from a broken neck. Nesbitt saw this and started pleading for his life. By now one of the giants, by the name of Running Bear, picked him up and threw him over to Big Eagle, who caught him with one hand. The tossing around went on for about fifteen minutes, and somewhere in those fifteen minutes Nesbitt died also from a broken neck. Taking both bodies and placing them into the hole dug by Jim and his compadres, the giants covered them over with dirt and when done stood there for a minute.

Red Hawk said as he looked at the little group, who were stunned with amazement at what they had just witnessed, "It's time for you to leave the valley and never come back. This place is sacred ground and you have done well in preserving the sacredness of the land.

"As you wish, we will leave tomorrow morning," Jim said, looking at Red Hawk.

Red Hawk smiled at Jim and the others, "You must tell no one of this place. The world isn't ready for this. The time will come when this place will be known, but not now."

"Yes, I understand."

Red Hawk, Big Eagle, and the others smiled at the group and walked away from them, with Big Eagle saying, "You know, all that work made me hungry. What's for dinner?"

Red Hawk laughed, "Everything makes you hungry."

"You noticed that too?"

As the four giants walked away to the cliffs where the burial chambers were, within minutes they were gone; and this time all the team saw them. Julie and the Dean, looking where the giants had gone, turned to look at Jim. "Who were those guys?"

"The guardians of the valley, I suppose."

Professor Wainwright smiled at Jim, "Those were the same guys that saved us the first time, weren't they?"

"Yes, as a matter of fact, they were, Professor."

"What do we tell the police about Jones and the man trying to kill us?" The Dean asked.

"What do you want to tell them, the truth?" Julie asked.

The Professor thought for a moment. "I didn't see a thing, how about you guys?"

All of them looked at each other and smiled. "See what?"

Walking back to their camp, the Professor asked all of them, "Did you see the headdress on the leader?"

"Yes," they all said.

"Just like the one in the coffin at the far end," Jim said.

As they thought about what had transpired, all of them were too excited to sleep for a while. They were talking about the size of the four Indians that had saved them. Eventually, as the night wore on, they started getting tired and drowsy as the excitement wore off. They crawled into their sleeping bags, turned off the lanterns, and went to sleep.

The next morning the team awoke to the sun shining, and after having breakfast they prepared to leave the valley for good. As they were about packed and ready to go, Red Hawk showed up again, this time not scaring Jim as bad. "I see that you are ready to go."

"As you have asked, we have done."

Red Hawk took Jim's hand to shake it. "This should make your journey easier to endure."

Holding Jim's hand, Red Hawk closed his eyes and proceeded to heal the wounded leg. Jim felt energized by what Red Hawk had done for him. Jim was surprised by this and Red Hawk laughed at him. "You white people are something else."

"You are too, my friend. Until we meet again," Jim said.

This time the old medicine man appeared, smiling, "Please return the medallion to the Utes."

"I will do that for you," Jim said.

The medicine man smiled as he looked at Jim and gave the hand sign of Go *in peace* and disappeared again.

All the others who saw this knew the next step was to find the rightful owner of the medallion. Putting their backpacks on, they headed out to get on the trail and hike back up the mountain, so they could reach their vehicles.

The trip took all of one day to get back to the Jeep and truck. When arriving at their vehicles, there was an old Indian standing off to the side of the trail waiting for them. Jim knew who it was and, walking over to the old Indian, took the medallion off and handed it to the Indian, who in turn thanked him for taking care of it and walked away. As Jim and the others watched the old Indian leave, they all knew the adventure was over for them, and all they would take with them would be the memories of what they had experienced. Unloading their gear into the back of the truck, they got into the Jeep and the truck and drove back to civilization.

Jim let Julie drive back to Salida, with Jim looking for a scar on his leg from the bullet and not finding one. Jim thought out loud, "I can't believe there is no scar; it's as if it never happened."

The Professor and the Dean were following close behind as they stopped in Salida once more to get gas and to find a room to clean up in. Soon they came out of their motel ready to eat.

They found a local café to eat at, walked in and sat down, and waited for the waitress to come over to take their food orders. Jim, looking at everybody, said, "I don't know about you guys, but I think I'll have a big bowl of baked beans for lunch."

They all gave out a groan and started laughing at Jim, with the waitress just standing there watching and smiling, not knowing what to say.

The End

Epilogue

Professor Wainwright stayed at the University until he retired. After the Dean retired, the Professor became the Dean and loved every minute of it.

The Dean stayed for another five years before retiring himself to become involved with finding more large skeletons in the surrounding area, specifically around Manti, Utah.

Jim became a Professor in good standing and worked at the university, taking a job which was left vacant by Professor Jones' unannounced departure.

Julie received her Ph.D. and became a Professor, teaching at the university as well. She and Jim had three kids and between her jobs, as a Professor and mother, she was very happy.

Professor Jones was never found, and nobody really missed him. Red Hawk made sure no one found his remains, having reburied them in a new cave near the end of the valley.

Nesbitt was never found as well, and nobody knew his real name or where he was from. He was reburied with Professor Jones in the same cave.

To this day no one talks much about their time in the valley in Colorado and, if they do, it's in the security of their homes, between themselves. All of them are hoping to be the ones allowed to discover the valley and show the world what they found there. They always end their conversations with "Someday, They Will Know."

It wasn't too much later, in fact, about a couple of years later, Jim had another dream, where Red Hawk came and visited him along with the medicine man.